LAP

ahea̶̶̶̶̶̶̶̶̶̶̶̶̶̶̶t.

̶̶̶̶̶̶̶̶e pricked his ears and scented the breeze.

̶̶̶̶̶̶̶̶̶̶̶̶̶ were few regular Cars on the roads — mostly, Shep saw the metal-box Cars — and what Cars he'd seen were driven by dog catchers.

The Car's doors flapped open.

I knew it. . . .

Two people, one with a pole and rope, climbed out. They began calling to Shep, whistling.

How much of a fuzz head do they think I am?

DOGS OF THE DROWNED CITY

DOGS OF THE DROWNED CITY

THE RETURN

DOGS OF THE DROWNED CITY

BY DAYNA LORENTZ

SCHOLASTIC INC.

NEW YORK TORONTO LONDON AUCKLAND
SYDNEY MEXICO CITY NEW DELHI HONG KONG

ISBN 978-0-545-27647-4

12 11 10 9 8 7 6 5 4 3 2 1   12 13 14 15 16 17/0

Printed in the U.S.A.   40
First printing, June 2012
Book design by Phil Falco

FOR TUI

CHAPTER 1
TRACKING CALLIE

Shep stood alone in the dark. There were no lights above him and no cage held him, but still he could not move. The cries of his friends echoed around him. Their voices moved like birds on the wind, but he saw nothing except the empty stone beneath his paws. He didn't know how to find his howling friends. He didn't know what he could do to save them. He stood, motionless, in the unending black.

A rumbling growl freed Shep from his nightmare. He cracked open his eyes just as one of the huge, squat metal-box Cars rolled past. These strange Cars and the green-clad humans who crouched inside them infested this part of the city. A dog could barely sneak a lap of water before some human showed up to snatch him.

Shep stretched from his shoulders to his claws. These new dreams were almost more terrifying than the old ones in which he was trapped in the fight cage or in the storm's wave. At least in those dreams, he knew what he had to do. Now, in his nightmares and his waking life, Shep was wandering blind, not certain of anything. He was far from every home he'd ever known, searching through a strange city for vanishing prey — his lost friends, his Callie.

But what other choice do I have?

The sun was setting, which meant that the remnants of Shep's pack — seven dogs and one cat — were due back from the sun's hunt. For the past three suns, the small pack had walked hundreds upon hundreds of stretches, from the boat toward the cold winds, looking for traces of the humans who had stolen their friends. Each sunrise, the dogs split up to search, going out alone or with one other dog. When the sun set, they met at a chosen landmark and then followed whatever trail had been found. It was a slow process, and a painful one: Every heartbeat lost to sniffing out the humans' scent was one more that the rest of his pack remained trapped. But Shep was adamant about taking these precautions. If he weren't afraid of losing the trail entirely,

2

he would forbid their moving when it was light out. He didn't want to lose another packmate to the dog catchers.

Shep rose and scented the late-sun air. He'd dozed in a moldy paper box after heartbeats of fruitless sniffing and now had to rush if he was going to rejoin his pack-mates at the meeting place by sunset. Just before dawn, they'd selected a ruined building with a tall, thin spire as a landmark; Shep hoped his wandering hadn't taken him too far from it.

He padded to the end of the alley. Long shadows stretched across the street. A dirty, tired-smelling woman pushed a cart filled with garbage bags along the Sidewalk. Shep decided that she didn't pose a threat and loped onto the open pavement.

His packmates were not as cautious as he was when it came to people. They seemed to have already forgotten the terrifying men in black who'd invaded the boat and taken their friends. Shep had not forgotten. In the suns since the invasion, he'd seen humans in normal-looking body coverings with long poles and dangling ropes chasing down strays. He warned the others that the dog catchers looked like every other person now. But did the pack listen to him? No, the fur-brains wagged their tails at every outstretched hand. They'd been lucky so far. Every evening, when all his dogs checked in at the meeting place, Shep gave thanks to the Great Wolf for their not having been captured, then reminded himself that there was no such phantom watching over them. No such thing as the Great Wolf. *Not anymore . . .*

A Car stopped ahead of him in the middle of the street. Shep paused; he pricked his ears and scented the breeze. There were few regular Cars on the roads — mostly, Shep saw the metal-box Cars — and what Cars he'd seen were driven by dog catchers.

The Car's doors flapped open.

I knew it. . . .

Two people, one with a pole and rope, climbed out. They began calling to Shep, whistling.

How much of a fuzz head do they think I am?

Shep wheeled on his paws and ran away down the pavement. He jumped through the broken front window of a building and hid behind a counter. Scenting the space, he smelled rot in the back corner. The back wall had partially collapsed and the ruined paper-stone was easily torn away. Shep scampered into a back alley and raced out onto an adjacent street. He dug his way under a wide plank of collapsed wall that rested on top of a Car and waited. His heart pounded and he panted hard.

4

Shep counted two hundred beats, then decided he was safe. He'd eluded his captors once again.

Boji and Dover were the first to reach Shep at the meeting place. The two Labs — one yellow like the morning sun and the other black as night — tended to go out together to search for their missing packmates. Boji was haunted by dark dreams of wounded and dying dogs. Dover, who always seemed to have his paws under him, stayed protectively by her side.

"Any luck?" Shep woofed. He himself hadn't found anything promising all sun.

"More humans," barked Dover. "And these weren't dog catchers. These were regular people. An old man and a young one helping the old to walk."

Boji loped over to Shep and gave him a friendly sniff. "Do you think this means our humans are back? Do you think we can go home?"

"I don't know," Shep answered. He didn't bother reminding Boji that her home had been torn apart by the storm, that even if she went back there, her family might never return to that pile of rubble. Instead, he woofed, "Even if your master were back, would you abandon your friends to the dog catchers?"

Boji's tail drooped. "You know that's not what I meant," she said. "I meant after we find them that we could go home."

Shep snorted. "Maybe," he woofed.

The pack members had been on this home topic ever since they saw the humans at the boat. All the woofs about home rubbed Shep's fur the wrong way. It wasn't just that he didn't think he had a den to go home to — Shep didn't *want* to go home. Sure, it would be nice to feel his boy's hand stroking his wet fur, rubbing him dry with a towel, and playing on the rug, but he couldn't give up barking with Callie every sun or running the streets with Blaze, hunting for rabbits. He had just gotten the pack going on the right scent when those dog catchers came in and ruined everything. He had to see what it was like to live free with his fellow dogs.

The rest of them would scent what Shep was smelling once the pack was together again. He knew it.

Rufus the schnauzer and Ginny the sheltie were the next to arrive. Shep never counted on them to find a useful track, but they usually returned with food. Shep had no time to hunt, so the pack ate whatever could be scavenged on the streets. Unfortunately, there wasn't much left on the street to scavenge. Ginny and Rufus, however, could always find something. This evening, they arrived with a bag of thick, circular pieces of bread.

"There seems to be more people in this part of the city," barked Ginny, "meaning much better pickings for food."

Shep's ears pricked. "Are you saying that you got this food from a human?"

Rufus wagged his tail — an unusually happy response from the squaredog. "You bet your tail we did!" he yapped. "Ginny stubbed her paw on a nasty bit of metal and was limping. This human saw her and made all sorts of cooing noises and dropped this bag at her paws."

Shep could hardly believe what he was hearing. "Are you positively out of your fur?" he bellowed. "That human could have snatched you up!"

Ginny stuck her snout in the air. "I think I can smell the difference between a human who wants to pet me and a human who wants to trap me," she growled. "This was a young girl, and she just wanted to stroke my brown fur, which, mind you, was a not uncommon occurrence before this horrible storm nonsense."

Shep didn't dig any further into the issue, sensing that he was the only dog in the room who felt that they should avoid all contact with humans. He munched his hunk of bread and watched the sky darken and worried whether any of the others would return.

Daisy the pug arrived with no new scent of their friends, but with similar stories of regular humans digging through the ruins of their dens or rolling around the streets in their Cars. Snoop the greyhound also had no luck.

"Sorry-Shep-all-I-smelled-was-humans-humans-everywhere-do-you-think-we-should-head-home-huh?" Snoop wagged his tail and had a hopeful look on his muzzle.

"No," Shep barked firmly. "Not until we rescue our friends."

Daisy slurped up the last crumb of her bread. "Do you still — *snort* — think we're going to find them?" she woofed. "It's been three whole suns, and the scent's been fainter with each passing of the moon."

"We are *going* to find them," Shep snapped.

Shep trotted to the hole in the den's wall to wait for his last two packmates — Oscar the dachshund puppy and Fuzz the cat. Every morning, Oscar raced out to search alone, sometimes not even waiting for every dog to wake before heading onto the streets. Perhaps the pup knew that none of the other dogs would have gone with him after how he'd betrayed the pack. Shep knew that Oscar was sorry for leading Zeus and the wild pack to the boat, that he never meant for the wild dogs to slaughter their friends. Shep had tried explaining this to the rest of the pack. But Higgins and Virgil had died, along with so many others — it was hard to forgive such a betrayal so soon after it had happened.

In other circumstances, Shep wouldn't have let Oscar go out alone. Fuzz seemed to have read Shep's thoughts. Every sun, after the pup scampered away from the den, the cat went out to shadow him. The fact that Fuzz always knew what was buzzing around in Shep's brain was some strange-smelling stuff that Shep would rather leave unsniffed. Whatever the reason for Fuzz's knowledge, Shep was glad that at least some dog — or cat — was looking out for the pup. Who knew what kind of trouble the misguided mutt would get them all into?

The fact that none of the dogs had found a scent was not good news. Boji and Dover had caught a trail on their search the sun before, and Snoop had found a scent the two suns before that. But Shep was not going to give up the search. He couldn't. Not after everything they'd been through. Not after he'd braved the fury of the storm, a pack of wild dogs, a world-crushing wave, and monstrous water lizards from the deep of the canal to collect this pile of dogs he called his pack.

*   *   *

The sun fell below the horizon and deep blue stretched over the roofs of the nearest buildings. Shep began to worry about the fur-brained pup. *What trouble has Oscar gotten himself into now?*

A Car squealed down the road and its headlights revealed Oscar's silhouette bounding toward the den.

"Shep!" he cried. "I found them!"

Shep's ears pricked up. "Where?"

The pup dragged himself through the hole in the wall, his thin tail whipping. "A little farther toward the cold winds," he woofed, panting. "I saw an open-backed Car with a dog in a crate. When it stopped, I ran up a pile of trash and jumped into the back with the other dog!"

Shep cocked his head. "You jumped into a dog catcher's Car?" he barked. "Have you lost your tail? We are trying to *rescue* dogs from the dog catchers, not give them easy prey!"

Oscar ducked away from him, but the grin on his jowls betrayed how happy he was that at least Shep was worried about losing him. The other pack members didn't seem to give a shed hair whether the pup was eaten by a water lizard.

"I was careful," Oscar woofed, trying to sound tough.

He explained that the truck drove toward sunset, then stopped at a big fence, beyond which sat huge Cars with stiff, birdlike wings on a field of pavement.

"I jumped out before the Car went into the fenced-in part, then ran back here. But I could smell that a whole mess of dogs were somewhere inside that place."

This was the best-smelling stuff Shep had heard in suns. "Do you remember how you got back here? Can you lead us to the field?" His tail was wagging so hard it hurt.

Oscar looked out the hole in the wall, then cocked his head. He sniffed the air. "I think so," he yipped. "Yes. Definitely. I think it's two streets up."

Daisy tilted her head to the side, unconvinced. "For all we know, the pup's leading us into another trap."

Oscar's tail drooped. "It's not a trap," he whimpered. "I promise on the Great Wolf's coat I'm telling the truth."

Dover raised his eyebrows, then looked at Shep and licked his jowls.

Fuzz materialized out of the evening shadows. "Big-ears-on-small-snout almost tell truth," he hiss-barked. He strutted into the midst of the dogs, swatting his long, fluffy tail. The cat explained how he'd followed Oscar and jumped onto the Car's bumper just before it growled away with Oscar in its back. "Fuzz keep careful track of trail between den and stone field. Three streets up, then many over. Pack together by sunrise."

Every tail wagged furiously, and the dogs yipped and barked with joy. Snoop slapped his paws on the ground and began to play with Boji and Dover. Fuzz sprang onto the back of a smashed wooden bench to avoid being crushed under the pounding paws. Rufus and Ginny bounded into the mix, snapping at the big dogs' jowls. Daisy stood to the side, yapping hysterically and flipping her knot-tail. Shep joined the game, nipping Boji's scruff and rolling onto his back. Then he saw Oscar sitting alone by the hole.

Shep stepped away from the scuffle and loped to the pup's side. "You made a great find, Oscar," he woofed. "You should celebrate." He bit one of the bread-rings Ginny had brought back and laid it at Oscar's paws.

Oscar glanced at the bread, then returned his gaze to the darkening street Outside. "I can't do anything right," he whimpered. "I find the others, but forget to keep track of the directions that would lead you all back there."

"But Fuzz remembered," Shep woofed, trying to

lighten the pup's black mood. "Everything is as well-furred as it could possibly be."

"For you," the pup replied. "For the pack, yes. But I need to do something. Something right, all by myself. Or else how can I ever expect any dog to forgive me?" He looked up at Shep with his huge, sad eyes. His ears hung limp around his muzzle.

"The pack will forgive you," Shep woofed, licking Oscar's head. "Just give them time."

CHAPTER 2
THE KENNEL

Shep allowed the others to take a short nap, just enough sleep to keep their paws moving under them. After the moon moved a stretch across the sky, he woke them and the pack set out to find the field of pavement crowded with winged Cars. The streets were dark — even though nearly two moon-cycles had passed since the storm, the city's lights were still out — and the dogs moved like shadows along the Sidewalk.

Shep kept his nose open for any humans. On previous nights, the pack had found sleeping men, and sometimes women and children, hidden inside paper boxes or even simply Outside under the Great Wolf's fiery coat, curled on the stone of the Sidewalk. Those humans must have returned to the city to find that their homes had been blasted apart by the storm or washed away by the wave.

When they found these denless humans, a part of Shep wondered about his boy, about whether his family slept on the stone in front of their broken den. And in that heartbeat, sadness exploded so violently inside Shep that he felt ready to burst. But he would wrestle himself back from those feelings. He had a pack to run. He had friends to rescue. He had a new life. He was the alpha.

Fuzz led the dogs under awnings and down alleys, careful to scent for any dangers. They were lucky to have the meower, though Shep knew most of the dogs would never admit to feeling that way. Even after all these suns, Shep himself was startled whenever the cat barked. Fuzz was eerily silent and still, and his eyes continued to set Shep's fur bristling when he caught their green glow flashing at him. It was weird living with a cat — they were just so different. But Fuzz had proved an invaluable pack member time and again.

When Shep allowed his mind to wander over his suns in the boat, he sometimes stumbled upon that wretched evening when he threw the cat out. In a heartbeat, all the horror that one stupid decision had led to would flood his memory. He would see poor Honey dead in that alley and his friends massacred by the wild dogs.

He would see Blaze's fierce eyes and cower all over again beneath their power. The guilt and anger and regret and sadness would tear through him like lightning.

Shep would dig through the memories, trying to find exactly where he'd gone wrong. He knew that if only he could track down exactly where he'd lost the right scent, he could ensure that he'd never make that mistake again. Once he had crushed that blunder in his jaws, Shep would become the alpha every dog needed him to be.

The first tails of dawn were flicking in the sky when the pack reached the fenced field of pavement. As Oscar had reported, tall Cars with stiff wings jutting from their backs were arranged in neat rows along the stone. Some were huge — bigger even than the boat! — others had blades like a ceiling fan where their noses should be.

The rows of bird-Cars stretched away from the fence that divided the dogs from the pavement field. Far down one row, Shep saw a building with a curved roof, like half of a giant tube. It was surrounded by bright white lights and what looked like stacks of crates. A strong scent of dog wafted from that direction.

Shep had to get to the tube building.

The fence protecting the field of pavement was tall and made of metal rings. The gate near the street was closed and held fast with thick chains and a lock.

Rufus poked the metal fence, rattling the rings. "The one thing we need to have been broken by the storm, and it's solid as stone," he grumbled.

"We can wait until the humans open the gate," woofed Boji, tail waving.

Daisy flopped into a sit. "You really think they're going to just — *snort* — let a bunch of strays wander into their fenced-in field?" she yapped.

"Smushed-snout correct," hissed Fuzz. "Truck stop at gate last sun, and human in small box on side of road check truck before let inside." Fuzz whipped his tail at the flimsy little building positioned alongside the road in front of the gate. "Dogs no get in this way."

"Then we'll have to find another way," Shep barked.

Shep waved his snout, and the dogs loped after him along the edge of the fence. Following the course of the fence led them away from the cold winds, then toward sunset, the fence curving to avoid a wide street. There were no other gates in the metal links, no weaknesses for the pack to exploit. Shep was losing all hope of finding a secret way into the field when they came across a toppled tree.

They were far from the gate now, and the sun shone above the steaming rooftops. Every dog was panting.

The tree had broken the top pole that held the metal fence up. The wall of rings was bent down nearly to the ground. Several sleeping winged Cars stood a few stretches from the fence, and beyond them, Shep could smell the dogs.

"Should we wait for night?" woofed Ginny, a hopeful look on her muzzle.

"No," Shep barked. "We need to check this building out now. But not all of us need to go. I'll scout the place out, then report back here with what I find."

"What should we do while you're gone?" woofed Dover.

"Stay hidden," Shep woofed. "I'll be back before midsun."

Shep hopped onto the tree trunk and crept along its length. The tree bounced on the metal of the fence, creaking loudly. Shep scrambled faster along the bark, then sprang over the fence and onto the pavement. Fuzz landed silently beside him.

"Fuzz keep Shep out of trouble," the cat meowed.

Shep waved his tail. "I didn't think you'd stay behind," he yipped. "Even if I nailed your tail to the street, I'd soon find you slinking in my shadow."

The cat closed his eyes and purred. "Perhaps it only Fuzz who see how lost dog-pack be without cat."

Shep panted. "It's not only you who sees that," he woofed.

"Watch out!"

Oscar plummeted from the tree and onto the cat's back with a crash. Fuzz let off an awful meow, then hissed something snarly in cat-speak.

"I thought I said I'd check things out while the rest of the pack stayed," Shep barked, annoyed. The last thing he needed was to have to keep track of the pup while sniffing out a dangerous nest of dog catchers.

"I won't get in your way," Oscar yipped. "And I found the place. I should get to check it out, too." He stood tall, his little chest puffed out.

Shep glanced at the others on the opposite side of the fence. Dover cocked his head and waved his tail, as if to say, Why fight the pup? Shep knew he would have to drag Oscar by the scruff back over the fence if he wanted him to stay put.

"Fine," Shep grumbled. "But keep right on my tail. I don't want to lose you in addition to every dog else."

The pup wagged his tail. "Don't you worry a hair about me," Oscar yapped. "I'll be right behind you."

Shep decided that they should approach the dog-smell building from the nearest row of winged Cars, so the three dashed across the pavement until they reached the belly of one of the massive metal birds. They crept from shadow to shadow, pressed close to one another, winding their bodies between the Cars' thin, metal legs. Then the bird-Cars ended.

About fifteen stretches of open pavement separated Shep from the first cage. In it lay a strange dog, big and brown — and asleep, though it was fully light out. On top of that cage was another, and another small crate rested on top of that. There were two cats in the second cage, a rabbit in the topmost. From this corner, the cages ran toward the cold winds and also toward sunset, farther than Shep could see. The smells of dog and cat and rat and rabbit and bird and Great Wolf knows what else bombarded his nose.

Oscar slumped beside Shep's forelegs, jaw slack beneath his jowls. "It's so big," he moaned. "How can there be so many dogs?"

Shep sat, unsure what else to do. This was too much, this kennel. How could they search all these cages? It would take a lifetime to sniff each one, to find all his packmates . . . to find Blaze . . . to find Callie.

"Fuzz look closer," the cat barked and burst from beneath the bird-Car. He stopped alongside the corner cage, then sprang onto the top of the first, then the second, and finally onto the roof of the third. The rabbit squealed and scrabbled around its little crate.

Fuzz raced along the tops of the cages and disappeared. Shep began to dig through his brain for how they could possibly invade this maze of crates, how best to find and free his friends.

"Down!" Oscar cried.

A small bus rumbled toward them along the space of pavement between the winged Car and the cages. Shep ducked deeper into the shadow, hiding himself. The bus drove halfway down the row of cages toward the building, then stopped. A door on its side slid open, and several humans in loose, colorful clothes stumbled out onto the pavement. This bus was followed by others — Cars (open backed and regular types) and all sorts of machines roared past, dropping off humans and a few dogs and other animals.

"This place is crawling with people," Shep mumbled to himself.

"But not at night," Oscar woofed. He squinted at the cages as if peering into the depths of the maze. "Everything is quieter at night. We could come back then and free all the dogs."

"Oscar, even if we worked from the heartbeat the sun set to when the first tails of dawn wagged, we couldn't open more than a snoutful of cages."

The pup glanced up at Shep. "A snoutful is better than none."

The sun baked the pavement. Heat rose in steamy waves from the stone. The dog in the corner cage finally woke and lapped up some water. Shep and Oscar stared at his bowl every time he slurped up a snoutful, their mouths dry as sand.

"Could you spare a drop?" Oscar barked to the strange dog. His tiny tongue stuck to the roof of his mouth, distorting his woof.

The dog glanced at him, then at the bowl. "Sorry," he yipped. "The human only comes by once a sun, and I only have enough water for me."

"Can you tell us anything about this place?" Shep woofed. "How many humans are here? How many dogs?"

The dog sniffed the air, then sat. "So many that I

never see the same human twice, and more dogs than I've ever smelled. They brought me here in this cage, and I've been in it ever since. Every afternoon, they take me for a walk by the edge of the fence, but other than that, what you see is what I see. Sometimes, strange humans walk by to peer into my cage, but not my girl. Not my family." Suddenly, the dog's ears pricked. He stood and waved his tail. "Have you seen my family out there?"

Shep sighed. "Sorry," he woofed. "I wouldn't know them even if I had seen them."

"But I'm sure they'll be here soon," Oscar added with a cheerful yip.

The dog's tail drooped. He lay down and rested his snout on his paws. "Yeah," he groaned. *"Soon."*

It was nearing midsun when Fuzz dropped down from the piles of cages and raced across the pavement to where Oscar and Shep lay panting in the shade.

"Took you long enough," Shep sighed. "We have to find some water."

"Fuzz find Callie-dog!" the cat meowed. "Callie-dog in building. Have tube in leg."

Shep sprang to his paws. "I'm going in," he woofed.

"Don't be a fuzz head," Oscar barked. "You'd be captured in a heartbeat." He bit Shep's foreleg for extra measure. "We have to find some water, meet back with the others, and come up with some plan that doesn't involve getting caught the heartbeat we set paw in the kennel."

Shep shook his fur, knowing Oscar was right but not liking a woof out of his snout. Callie was here! Callie was in trouble! He had to save her!

"Small-snout right." Fuzz flicked Shep in the nose with his tail. "Shep-dog wait. No help to Callie-dog with fur-for-brain."

They made their way as fast as their paws could manage back to the fence. As they walked, Fuzz explained what he'd seen in the complex.

"Cages in rows, piles of cages. Rodent on cat on dog on dog." His disgust at the arrangement was evident in the tone of his hiss. "But in building, less cages and less dogs. More people. Callie there."

Shep pressed Fuzz for better details of the space, but the cat had little to offer.

"Fuzz no have time to scratch out plan of whole space," he meow-barked. "If Shep-dog want explain better, he go sniff out building himself."

"Then that's what I'll have to do," Shep grumbled.

The others were waiting on the other side of the fence around the toppled tree trunk. It looked like in all those heartbeats, they hadn't moved a paw.

"What did you — *snort* — find?" barked Daisy.

"Yeah-Shep-did-you-find-Callie-and-can-we-go-home-yet-huh?" Snoop leapt against the metal rings of the fence and sent the whole wall shivering.

Rufus nipped Snoop in the hind leg. "Get down before you set the whole mess of humans on us!" he snapped.

Shep smelled that the pack was feeling equal parts anxious and excited. "Did something happen while I was gone?"

"Humans," woofed Dover. "A few drove by in one of those open-backed Cars. They marked the tree." He waved his nose, and Shep saw an orange X painted on the trunk.

Daisy pawed closer to Shep, chest out like she was trying to appear taller. "I ordered the pack to jump into a bush," she grunted. "We stayed hidden."

Daisy was all that was left of Shep's defense team, and apparently she thought this meant that she was in charge when he was away. If the others didn't raise their hackles over the arrangement, Shep wasn't going to make anything of it.

He wasn't sure why the humans painted a mark on the tree, but it couldn't be for anything good. Shep had to get his trapped packmates out of this place and fast.

"We found Callie, so the others can't be far," barked Shep. "Our pack will be back together by sunrise."

The dogs moved away from the fence for the rest of the afternoon, not wanting to attract any more attention to their entry-tree. They began searching the gully alongside the wide street for water and food, and found a few slurps and bites to swallow down.

Daisy strutted to Shep's side. "What's the rescue plan?" she yapped.

"Fuzz found Callie in the tube building," Shep woofed. "We start there, and then open as many cages as we can on our way out."

Daisy gave Shep a snaggletoothed head tilt. "Not to smell insubordinate, but that's all you've got for a plan?"

"I didn't sniff out the place; Fuzz did." Shep turned over a moldering box and found only more trash. "When we go back in tonight, I'll get a scent for how the whole kennel is set up and think of something better."

Daisy snorted and kicked back in the dust. "Blaze was better at this than you are," she barked. "Callie, too."

"Thanks, Daisy," Shep growled.

"And Virgil."

"I said *thanks*."

Shep spent the rest of the afternoon digging around his brain for a better plan, something to shove Daisy's snout in, but nothing came to him. He was the kind of dog who worked best in the heartbeat — he was a doer, not a thinker. But he didn't have Callie to think for him now. He had to think for both of them, to save her.

It would be silly to bring every dog in with him to investigate the building — better for only him to get caught than the whole pack. He could sniff things out with Fuzz as lookout, and probably Oscar, since the pup was such a stubborn tick in the fur. The rest could wait by the fence until he had a plan in place. Something even better than what Blaze would have come up with. Probably not as good as what Callie would have thought up, but something.

As the sun began to fall, Shep barked that they should head back to the fence.

"Wait!" howled Ginny. "I've found a den!"

She stood in front of a huge tube, a stretch across at least. It was similar to the tunnel Shep had played in at the Park. The tube seemed to run under the wide street, though Shep could barely see through to its end in the dying light.

"We'd better sniff this out," he woofed.

The dogs were wary of setting paw in the tube — it was dark, and it smelled terrible. A trickle of grimy water ran along its bottom and the metal under the water was coated in a thick layer of slime. Shep longed for Callie to appear beside him, to see her run headlong into the tube out of sheer curiosity. *Soon*, he told himself. *She'll be back with me soon.*

"Last dog through is a soggy kibble," Shep woofed and raced into the dark.

The tunnel led into a wooded area, and the trickle of water opened into a wide, shallow stream. The dogs followed the stream through the trees. The water grew deeper, and Shep saw at its end an open expanse of water surrounded by fields.

"It's a Park," he barked. His tail began to wave in wide circles. "Perfect!"

Dover sniffed at a wallow of mud. "Water lizard," he yipped. "And something else. Both were here not too long ago." He pricked his ears. "We're not alone in this Park."

"We don't have to be alone," Shep said, tail still in full swing. "I'm the alpha of any water lizard or nasty rodent we find. The real nugget is that there aren't any dog catchers in this Park. It's separate from the fenced pavement field. We can free the dogs and then meet back here."

"So how exactly do we free the others?" yapped Rufus. "I don't know about you, but I don't think I can open any cages with my paws or my teeth."

The other dogs looked at Shep with raised ears, eager to hear what he'd woof. Daisy gave him her usual head tilt, this time with a distinct snarl of disapproval.

Shep snorted and pawed the ground. "Well," he began, "first, I'm going to go in and check the place out. Then I'll come up with the plan. And then we'll execute the plan."

"All in one night?" woofed Boji. She waved her tail, but the look on her muzzle betrayed her doubts.

"Yes," Shep barked as assuredly as he could. "They'll all be free by next sun."

Fuzz leapt down from the tree branch he'd been perched upon. "Enough barking. Dogs need to move tail if finish before sun time."

CHAPTER 3
ESCAPE

The sun burned low on the horizon, setting the clouds on fire against the pale blue of the fading sky. Already, a lone flame of the Great Wolf's coat flickered in the dark. The pack agreed to wait by the tree until Shep returned with his rescue plan. As Shep had anticipated, Oscar refused to stay behind, so the pup and the cat followed Shep to the maze of cages.

The humans had lit tall, blinding white lights near the curved-roof building as the sky grew dark; however, their light didn't penetrate all the way to the outer cages. The three invaders were able to hide in the shadows all the way to the opening in the maze where they'd seen people dropped off that morning. As they crept along, Shep sniffed each of the cages, but nothing smelled familiar. *Not that I'd recognize the scent of most of my pack,* he reminded himself. By the time the catchers had come to the boat, the pack had grown so large that Shep hadn't known every dog.

Shep peeked around the edge of the last cage and got his first look inside the maze. His jaw dropped. There were more cages, endless cages — row after row, piled on top of one another, some with one dog, others with as many as three.

Oscar whined, "How will we ever find our pack in this place?"

"Dogs, focus," Fuzz hissed. "This way to Callie-dog." He flicked his tail and slunk through the shadows toward the building.

Shep and Oscar followed, pressed to the side of the row of cages. Every once in a while, a captured dog would snap at them from inside the crate, but for the most part, the strangers merely sniffed them, tails wagging. Some asked about their families, whether they'd seen a certain girl with red pigtails like floppy ears or a man with curly brown hair. Shep tried to block out their questions; every woof pulled at him like a thorny branch. He wanted to help them, but that's not why he was there, not now. Now he needed to save Callie.

Fuzz hissed for them to stop several stretches away

from the building. The lights scared away every shadow. The three had nowhere to hide.

"Shep-dog get good enough scent of place?" Fuzz meowed. "Time to move tail out of maze." The cat stared at Shep, but his ears flicked nervously, catching every sound.

"Hey, dog!" a human voice called.

Shep froze. He glanced around him, twitching his ears to catch where the voice came from.

"Here, boy," the voice said, closer.

Shep saw the person — a young man in pale blue body coverings — two rows over, kneeling in front of a cage. He dragged behind him a bag of kibble, the scent of which set Shep's mouth slobbering.

"Quick," Shep snuffled. "Pad backward until we hit shadow, then bolt for the opening in the maze."

They made it out onto the open pavement and under one of the winged Cars without getting caught, but this did not make Shep any more relaxed.

"It's not that there are no humans here at night," he grumbled. "There may be fewer, but there are still enough to catch every one of us."

"Shep-dog should forget plan," Fuzz meow-barked. "Callie-dog safe. Those humans smell good, take care of dogs."

Shep glared at the furball. "I made a promise to Callie. I'm not going to give up on her."

Fuzz licked a paw and ran it over his ears. "Fine," he hissed. "But Shep-dog do rescue for Callie or for self?"

Shep kept his snout shut. He agreed with the cat that the humans seemed to be helping the pets in the cages. At least these dogs had eaten a decent meal this sun, which was more than any in his pack could woof. But these dogs were still in cages and not with their families. Shep felt in his gut that they would all rather be free like he was.

Oscar peered around the metal-stick leg of the winged Car. "What's going on over there?" he woofed.

On the other side of the maze of cages was a huge winged Car — better to call it a winged den, it was so big. There was a hole in the den's body near its tail and a ramp led from the pavement into the hole. At the base of the ramp was a pile of crates, each filled with a barking dog. The ramp must have had some special rug on it: A human placed a cage containing a small, brown dog onto the ramp and the crate was carried up the ramp and into the winged den.

"Why would they put the dogs into the big Car?" Oscar whimpered.

"I don't know," moaned Shep, though he worried it couldn't be for anything good.

"Winged Cars fly," Fuzz meowed. "Take dogs far away."

Shep stared at the cat. *How does he know that?* "You mean, like a bird?"

"Fuzz owner take Fuzz on fly-Car to get Honey-friend as puppy," he hissed. "Fuzz not happy in fly-Car." He gagged slightly as if choking back a hairball.

Oscar began to tremble. "Why would they send the dogs away?" he whined. "What about their families?"

"There must be too many of them to care for here," Shep woofed. He straightened his stance, ears up and tail lifted. He wasn't just doing this for himself. He had to keep the humans from taking Callie away from her home.

"It's too risky to bring Daisy and the others in here," Shep barked. "But we need to get Callie out before they fly her away in that fat bird-Car." He glanced back at the cage maze. "Here's the plan — Oscar, you and Fuzz head for the building and get Callie out. I'm going to create a distraction down here. All the humans should come running to me, and that will give you at least a few heartbeats to escape with Callie."

"Has Shep-dog completely lost brain?" Fuzz roared. "Humans take Shep-dog for sure with that fuzz-head plan."

"But you'll get Callie out, which is all I care about."

The humans loaded the last cage into the bird-Car. A man shouted and a little Car pulling a flat, wheeled trailer drove back into the maze — *to get more.*

Shep growled softly. "We have to do this now."

"I'll create the distraction," Oscar barked. "You go and get Callie out."

"No, pup," Shep grunted. "You won't be able to cause half the ruckus I can."

"I don't need to do anything except annoy the biggest dog I can find," Oscar snapped. "And I'm really good at annoying big dogs. As you should know." He gave Shep a fierce look. "Please, let me do this. I need to do this, to prove I can be a good packmate."

"Oscar," Shep woofed, "how many times have I told you — you don't need to prove anything. And I will figure a way to get myself out of here."

"The pack can't lose you," Oscar said. "They don't need me. They don't even want me. But they'll be lost for sure without you." He pricked his ears and lifted his chest. "Plus, I'm small. If I create a big enough mess, I can slip away without the humans seeing me."

"Small-snout correct," Fuzz hissed. "Shep-dog come with Fuzz. Let pup do bark-and-bite distraction."

Oscar's woofs made sense, but Shep felt like a coward, letting the pup run full-snout into danger alone.

Then again, who knew what challenges he would face in the building trying to free Callie? Shep could cause a distraction and get caught, and the pup might not be able to reach Callie's cage to open it. No, Oscar was right. He had a good plan.

"Okay," Shep woofed. "But you meet me back in the Park, pup. No unnecessary heroics."

Oscar sprang up and licked Shep's nose. "Oh, thank you!" he howled.

"All right," Shep yipped. "Quiet down before we both get snatched."

Oscar shut his jaws, though his jowls remained curled in a huge grin. He wagged his tail, then bounded into the dark to search out a cage full of angry big dogs.

"Fuzz lead," the cat meowed.

"No," Shep woofed. "Go back to the fence and tell the others the plan. Have them head into the Park and mark a trail with scent, then wait for us there. If the humans follow us, I don't want them stumbling upon the whole pack at the fence. Best to keep the others safe in case Oscar and I need rescuing."

Fuzz considered Shep's woofs for a heartbeat, then nodded his pink nose and disappeared into the black.

Time for a daring rescue.

*   *   *

The moon was high in the sky. Shep crept through the shadows along the edge of the maze. He slipped through the hole they'd found in the outer wall of cages, making his way back toward the tube building. The artificial light from the humans' lamps soon drowned out the silver light of the moon. Shep had to step out into the brightness, leaving the protection of the shadows.

He sniffed the air, though all he could scent was dog and the occasional cat or rodent. He had to trust that there were no humans nearby. He kept low to the ground and scuttled forward across an open path between the cages.

The closer he got to the building, the fewer obstacles he had to hide behind. Then the maze of cages ended. All that separated Shep from the building was an open stretch of pavement. A few Cars slept near the building. In the open space were three large tents under which were crowded plastic tables and chairs. A few humans loitered by one of the tables, staring at a small lightwindow and shuffling piles of paper.

Shep dashed from his cover and dove under one of the Cars. His body was pressed between the metal belly of the Car and the pavement, but he managed to scooch his way to the front of the Car.

He was now only a stretch away from the outer wall of the building. The tube building itself was open. White lights lined its spine from front to back. There were rows of cages inside, and between each row was a shiny, metal table with boxes and bins stored beneath it. A light hung from a metal arm over each table.

The pets in the cages here were hooked up to beeping human machines or bags and tubes or both. Some were wrapped in strips of cloth, but most lay limp in their cages on ragged towels.

Shep stole from beneath the Car to the edge of the row closest to the outer wall.

"Callie?" he snuffled.

The dog nearest him — a medium-sized black dog, probably a pit bull like Paulie — lifted his snout. "What are you doing out of your cage?" he growled.

"Have you seen a little dog, brown with a black muzzle?" Shep woofed.

The black dog panted. "You must've grown fur on your brain," he yipped. "What kind of dog *haven't* I seen?"

"Thanks," Shep grumbled. "You've been extremely helpful."

Shep padded along the row until there was a break in the cages. A path led from the outer row all the way across the building. In the center of the building, Shep saw a plastic table with a few plastic chairs — and the legs of a human stretched out in front of one of the chairs.

Where's my big distraction, Oscar? Shep grumbled to himself.

Shep crept along the central path, woofing Callie's name up and down each aisle. When he reached the center of the building, he saw that the legs belonged to a young woman who was fast asleep in the chair. Her head rested along the thin rim of the plastic back and her arms hung limp, draped over the armrest.

It was the closest Shep had been to a human since the storm. A part of him was desperate to nuzzle under her sleeping arm, to feel her hand stroke his fur. He could hardly remember what it felt like to have someone scratch behind his ears. Suddenly, that one bit of skin that he could never scratch properly flared up.

"Shep?"

He turned his snout. And there she was.

Callie's muzzle lit up like a lamp. "Shep!" she yipped. "It's really you!"

Shep trotted to her cage. Callie leapt up on her hind legs. She licked the metal bars and waved her tail ecstatically.

"How did you find me?" she woofed, catching his jowl with her lick. "They took me so far from the boat, I figured I was lost forever."

"If they'd taken you all the way to the Silver Moon, I'd have found you," Shep yipped, licking her through the bars.

Callie looked past his ears, then pulled a tube out of her leg with a wince. "We have to hurry," she snuffled. "They're moving the whole kennel, I think. I've seen them looking over lists and loading dogs into that big winged Car."

"Just let me slap open this cage," Shep woofed and began digging with his claws at the latch.

"Shep," Callie woofed in a solemn tone, "they already took Blaze."

The name hit him like a rolled newspaper. *Blaze is gone. . . .* He closed his eyes. *She won't ever see her man again, or her beasts. I won't ever get to see her again.* He felt awful that their last woofs to each other had been hurtful; they'd never even gotten to wag tails good-bye. The sadness welled up inside him like a black pool. *No,* he commanded. *I must stay strong. I have to save Callie.*

"She was flown out last sun." Callie nuzzled his paw. "I'm so sorry."

Shep licked his jowls. "There's nothing we can do about that," he yipped. "The important thing is to rescue you."

The dog in the cage next to Callie threw herself against the metal-mesh wall, sending the whole row rattling. Shep glanced at the human. She groaned in her sleep, then snored on.

"Are you trying to get me caught?" he snapped at the dog.

The dog — a small white thing, poodle or shih tzu or something like that — began whimpering pathetically. "I heard you say 'rescue,' and I need you to rescue me, too, please?" She batted her big black eyes. "I need to get home to my mistress and they said my name when they read the last list and I can't go away from my mistress, PLEASE? I'm so small you'd never even notice me, pleasepleaseplease*PLEASE*!"

Shep dragged the latch on Callie's cage and the door swung open.

"Be quiet!" he growled. "If you shut your snout, I'll open your cage."

The little dog began furiously wagging her tail. "Oh, thankyouthankyouthankyou, you big wonderful fabulous furry ball of snuggleliciousness!"

"Pumpkin, you're being a little dramatic," Callie grumbled. She pawed the air in front of her cage as if a staircase might magically appear from her cage to the ground.

"No, I'm being grateful," the small white dog — Pumpkin — woofed.

"Be grateful a little more quietly," Shep snuffled. "We don't want to wake up that human."

Shep dug open Pumpkin's cage, and the little girldog flounced out onto the ground. Callie, however, was still pawing at the air.

"Need help?" Shep woofed, smirking.

"Don't make fun," Callie yipped. "I'm recovering from a severe injury."

Shep gripped her by the scruff and dropped her on the ground.

"Hey," woofed a large brown dog a few cages away. "What about me?"

"And me!" yapped a little black-and-white mutt. "Rescue me!"

Every dog started to bark like a crazy thing. The human stirred in her chair.

"Shut your snouts!" Shep growled as quietly as he could.

Just then, Shep heard a loud crash and a chorus of barks and snarls.

"That'll be Oscar," Shep woofed.

"Oscar?" asked Callie. "What's he got to do with anything?"

The woman woke; her eyes locked on Shep.

"Don't ask," Shep barked. "Just run."

The human stood and placed her hands in front of her. She spoke in a calm voice, then turned her head and yelled something.

"Run, Callie!" Shep barked. He sprang off his hind legs and hit the woman in the chest, knocking her back into the table. He stuck his head under the edge of the plastic top and tipped the whole table onto its side.

The woman screamed. Shep heard other human voices shouting.

"What are you doing?" Callie cried. "She helped me — and you hurt her!"

"Never mind! We have to leave now!" Shep snapped. He nudged Callie in the side, and they took off down the aisle toward the wall.

"More people are coming!" Pumpkin yapped as she raced by Shep.

Shep turned at the wall and bolted for the open end of the building, then noticed Callie was no longer beside him. He glanced back and saw the little girldog huffing around the corner at a trot.

"You have to go faster!" Shep barked.

"This is as fast — *pant pant* — as I go," Callie groaned, catching up to him.

They would never outrun whatever humans were after them, loping along at Callie's pace. He needed more of a distraction.

"You keep heading down that aisle at the edge of the cage maze," Shep barked.

"And you?" Callie yipped.

"I'm going to cause some trouble."

A person with a long pole and rope stepped from between the row of cages a few stretches from where Shep and Callie stood.

"Don't hurt him!" Callie yelped.

"Get going!" Shep snapped at her.

He turned to face the person. The man was talking slowly in a low voice and creeping toward Shep. The aisle was empty — there was nothing for Shep to do but attack. He lunged back, preparing to ram the man, and noticed a tower of lights. Its two square lamps buzzed three stretches above Shep atop a thin stick. *Now there's a distraction.*

Shep bolted out of the building and slammed his paws against the lights. The tower wobbled on its base, which was like a metal bird's foot, then crashed to the pavement. The bulbs burst, sending up a shower of glass shards and throwing the area into darkness.

The man yelled, but Shep didn't stop. He bolted into the dark and followed Callie's scent out of the maze of cages. He paused to catch his breath under one of the small, sleeping winged Cars.

Callie stumbled to his side. "Please — *pant* — tell me you didn't attack the man," she woofed.

"I attacked a light," Shep grunted.

"Why — *pant* — did you hit the woman?" she whimpered. "She was a nice person."

"She was going to put us all in cages and send us Great Wolf knows how far from our homes."

Shep's bark sounded more confident than he felt. Actually, he was shivering under his fur. He didn't need Callie to tell him he'd done something bad; every hair in his body felt tingly, like his coat was trying to get as far from him as possible. He had hit so many dogs and other animals in their chests to defend himself — why did hitting the woman feel so different?

Pumpkin appeared under the winged Car. "I think we're safe," she woofed. "The humans ran away from the building, down a different aisle."

"What was Oscar doing?" asked Callie.

"He was creating a distraction so we could get away," Shep barked. "So let's get our tails out of here."

Shep led Callie and Pumpkin to the tree, over the fence, and along the scent trail left by the others through the tunnel into the Park. The dogs were silent as they ran; the only noises were the twitch of leaves on the tree branches and the splash of water echoing around the inside of the tube. When they exited the tunnel, they found the rest of the pack waiting in the dim moonlight, huddled near the tunnel's opening.

"Shep?" woofed Ginny, her bark weak and trembling.

"It's me," he answered, "and I have Callie."

Callie stood tall and waved her curly tail. Boji padded out of the shadows, her tail wagging, and gave Callie a good licking.

"You smell better," Boji woofed.

"I am better," Callie said, turning her head slightly so Boji could lick her ear. "Smell how clean it is? The humans fixed my stomach from that nasty plant, and they even stopped my ears from itching." Callie cut her woofs short, glanced at Shep, and sat. "The humans were helping the hurt dogs."

Fuzz sat beside Shep's flank and twitched his ears.

"Shep-dog try to help," he hissed. "Callie-dog like it in cage so much she can go back."

"Fuzz," Shep groaned, though it was nice to hear at least some dog — cat — supporting him. Callie sounded like she would have rather stayed in the kennel.

Callie's ears flapped around her jowls. "I don't mean it that way," she woofed. "They were flying dogs far away. I saw them load Blaze and some of the others from our pack into one of those big winged Cars, and it growled and screeched and then blasted off into the air. I don't want to leave the city." She licked her nose. "I just think we need to remember that the humans aren't our enemies."

She gave Shep another look — like he didn't know humans weren't enemies, like he didn't feel terrible about having hurt that woman.

Daisy stood and stretched. "Of course — *snort* — they're not. Who said they were?" She shook her fur and kicked back with her hind legs. "Now, what about the others?" she barked. "What about Hulk and Panzer?" She wagged her knot-tail as if those big dogs from the defense team were her real packmates.

"We didn't have time to rescue any others," Callie yipped. "There were too many humans."

"Not true!" yipped Pumpkin. "One other! Don't forget me!" The tiny ball of fluff raced into the circle of dogs, then rolled and slapped the dirt with her front paws and barked, then zipped into the shadows and back out again into the circle of dogs. "Hi! I'm Pumpkin!" She waved her tail, which was bony with a tuft of long hairs on its end. "I'm a champion purebred Havanese show dog!" She sprang into the air, then panted happily as she pranced in a circle.

Daisy gave Pumpkin a severe head tilt, so far that Shep worried her neck might snap, but the others grinned, amused by the little dog's antics. Shep wanted to slam a paw down on the fluffy white yapper's back to keep her from moving, and panted to himself, thinking that Zeus would have done exactly that.

And then, as if Shep's thoughts had been made real, Zeus himself hobbled out of the tunnel and into a beam of moonlight.

"Hello, old friends," the boxer growled.

CHAPTER 4
DECISIONS, DECISIONS

Zeus lowered his hornlike ears. "What?" he grunted. "No wag for your old packmate?"

"Get back!" Shep snapped, raising his hackles and sinking into a defensive stance.

The pack scrambled to get behind Shep. Daisy stood at his flank, ears up and fangs bared. Dover stood at Shep's other flank, a low growl rumbling in his throat. Even Boji — gentle, scaredy-dog Boji! — snarled at the boxer.

"Do I need to remind you that I banished you from my pack?" Shep growled.

"No," Zeus barked, sneering. "I carry around a constant reminder." He lifted his front paw. It was wrapped in a heavy bandage that thudded against the dirt when he dropped the leg. "Apparently, though, you didn't share that woof with every dog in your pack." Zeus flicked his muzzle back toward the dark of the tunnel.

"I told you to wait!" Oscar's bark echoed out at them. The pup appeared, covered in muck, and shook his coat, splattering Zeus with mud. "They didn't know you were coming," he woofed to the boxer, as if the whole pack weren't right in front of him.

"Of all the dogs to rescue!" Ginny cried. "Have you forgotten what he *did*?"

"No dog's forgotten," Callie barked, her voice flat. A scowl bent her jowls and the front of her lip trembled over her bared teeth.

Pumpkin popped out from between Dover's legs. "What'd he do?" she yipped. "He looks hurt."

"I killed their friends," Zeus answered. His sonorous bark hung in the thick air under the trees.

"Oh," woofed Pumpkin. "I can see why they're upset."

"Oscar," Shep growled, "what is he doing here?"

The pup trotted under Shep's snout to explain; Shep kept his eyes trained on Zeus.

"I did just what we planned," Oscar woofed. "I sniffed for a good cage to attack to cause the ruckus we had woofed about, a cage with a couple of big dogs in it.

I thought that if there were a few big dogs, then maybe they would attack each other as well as the cage and maybe that would make more ruckus, and I thought the more ruckus the better, right?"

"Get to the point, pup," growled Dover.

Oscar glanced nervously at Dover. "Well, so I was sniffing, and then this dog — it was Zeus! — barked my name, and I was all, 'Hey, I'm mad at you!' and he was all, 'I'm mad at myself, is Shep around, I want to ask him to forgive me,' and so I was all, 'Well, he's not *here*, but he's around,' and so Zeus promised to help me make a ruckus if I led him back here so that he could ask you for forgiveness."

"Some dog — *snort* — better get this mutt out of my sight before I start to get nasty," Daisy snarled.

"Wait!" howled Oscar. "Zeus just wants to ask you all to forgive him. Give him a chance to explain himself!"

"Nothing he barks is going to make any difference," woofed Shep.

Zeus grimaced at Shep's woofs. "I just came here to tell you that I'm sorry. I'm sorry for everything."

Fuzz sprang onto Dover's back, hackles shivering along his arched spine. "Zeus-dog never forgiven!" he shrieked. "Zeus-dog kill Honey-friend!"

Shep nodded to Fuzz. "Don't worry, Fuzz," Shep woofed. "He's not staying."

The cat lowered his spine but kept his tail up and twitching.

Shep turned back to Zeus. "I don't want your sorry," he snapped. "I want Higgins and Virgil and Honey back." Shep stood tall, rising out of his defensive pose. "What you did can never be forgiven."

In his gut, Shep sensed that Zeus didn't mean what he'd woofed about being sorry. Something about the glint of light in his eye and the tone of his bark told Shep that his former friend was here for something, and it wasn't an apology. Shep's gut said that Zeus was here to finish what he'd started. Shep couldn't take the chance of trusting Zeus's woofs, not after everything he had done. Zeus wasn't worth the trouble.

The boxer sank back into a sit. He licked his jowls, as if considering Shep's barks. "Well," he woofed, "then I'm sorry I upset you by coming here." He turned away and stepped back into the tunnel.

"No," barked Oscar. "Don't go." The pup looked at his packmates, still huddled behind Shep. "What more do you want Zeus to woof? He said he's sorry, he said he wants to be good. Can't a dog want to change?" He stood tall — as tall as he could — and barked in a firm voice, one much more adult than Shep expected from the pup. "If you can forgive me, you have to be able to forgive Zeus."

No dog so much as snuffled.

Oscar gazed into each of their muzzles, ending on Shep's snout. Oscar's large eyes searched Shep's. Shep tried to hide his feelings, but something must have slipped. Oscar looked away.

"So you haven't forgiven me," he grunted. "Not even you, Shep."

"We're all trying," woofed Shep.

"Fuzz not trying," hissed Fuzz, who still shivered with rage.

Shep shot the cat a that's-not-helping look. "Most of us are trying," he barked, turning back to Oscar and licking the pup on the head. "But Zeus is a different scent entirely. You may have done something completely fur-brained, but Zeus killed our friends." Shep glared at the boxer.

"I don't care what you do," Shep barked to Zeus. "But you can't stay in my pack. If you're waiting for your human to return, do it somewhere else."

Pumpkin's little white head popped out again from behind Dover. "Return?" she yipped. "The humans aren't going to return."

"Hush up, dear," yapped Ginny. "Shep's in the middle of a speech."

"But he's wrong," whined Pumpkin. "The humans can't return because they never left!"

Suddenly, every muzzle was on the tiny fluff of fur.

"What-does-she-mean-Shep-we-all-saw-our-humans-leave-and-we-never-scented-them-when-we-were-in-the-city —" Snoop cut his rambling bark off and stared wide-eyed at Pumpkin. "Do-you-know-where-my-master-is?" he asked, almost slowly enough to be intelligible.

Pumpkin popped up on her paws like a frog, frisking and flopping with excitement. "You didn't know?" she yipped. "Oh my goodness, I can't believe you didn't know!"

Callie padded closer to Pumpkin, eyebrows raised and tail waving cautiously. "How do *you* know that the humans never left?" she woofed. "My girl and her family locked me in my den and I haven't had a whiff of them since."

Pumpkin sat, head tilted. "They left you *behind*?" she barked. Her snout dropped against her chest dramatically. "Shave my fur and call me a squeaky toy." She shook herself and continued, "No, my mistress hid me in a bag and carried me with her to this building, far from our den. There were all these other people crowding to get into the building, and there were people in green body coverings standing at the door checking each person in. They kept saying 'shelter,' and so that's what I call the place.

"Inside, there were rows and rows of narrow beds for the humans. My mistress hid the bag I was in under her bed. I wanted to get a look around, you know, to see what this shelter was, so I dug my way out. Just as I was about to scramble under the next bed over, one of those green people saw me and started yelling. I tried to run, but the green woman was too fast and she snagged me around my belly. My mistress screamed and cried and I wriggled, trying to get back to her to comfort her, but the green woman just took me and handed me off to some other green person, and I ended up at that kennel you rescued me from."

"Why were you in the medical tent?" yipped Callie.

Every dog was on the tips of his pads, leaning toward her with ears pricked and eyes open wide. Shep held his breath, not wanting to miss a woof.

"I kept breaking out of my cage," said Pumpkin, sighing. "They moved me there so that they could keep an eye on me. And then I hurt my leg breaking out of yet another cage. They had to sew me up like a toy. Can you believe it? But I had to get free and get back to my poor mistress. She's positively *lost* without me. And now that I'm out, I can take you all with me to the shelter. We can find our humans!"

The pack burst into a riot of happy howling. They jumped and barked and batted at each other's muzzles. Shep remained frozen on his paws. His boy was in the city. His family had stayed. *But if they stayed, why did they leave me alone to be eaten by the storm?*

Zeus snuffled from behind him, "I can't imagine going back to my collar." His voice, dripping with disgust, echoed in the tunnel.

It struck Shep as the saddest of jokes that Zeus was the only dog whose thoughts matched his own. How could he go back to a family that abandoned him? Especially when he felt so alive living on the Outside. Yes, he missed his boy, but there was so much more of the world to explore!

Callie barked for every dog's attention. "We're not back with our humans yet," she woofed. "Pumpkin, how far is it to the shelter? Can we be there by morning?" Her tail whipped behind her ecstatically.

Pumpkin stopped mid-bounce, flopping back to the ground. She looked around at the darkness of the scrubby woods, then back at Callie. "It's not far from my den," she yipped.

"Where's your den?" woofed Boji, tail wagging. "Nearby?"

Pumpkin sank into a sit. "No," she snuffled. "They put me in a Car to take me here, and we drove for many heartbeats."

"Then why'd you get our tails up?" snapped Rufus. "What use is knowing our humans are *somewhere* in the city? We always knew they were somewhere." The squaredog stomped into the shadows.

Ginny, who'd begun to whine pathetically, skittered after him into the dark.

"Keep within the scent perimeter!" barked Daisy, strutting after the others.

"I'm sorry!" whimpered Pumpkin. "Maybe if we all go back to my den, I can lead you there?"

She waved her tail, but no dog would return her wag. The rest of the pack returned to the nests they'd made in the dead leaves and bracken. Only Pumpkin, Shep, Oscar, and Zeus were left in the clearing.

"I only want to get home," moaned Pumpkin. "Won't any dog help me get home?"

"Let's see how the fur falls in the morning," Shep

woofed. He didn't mention how relieved he was that Pumpkin couldn't just wave her tail and lead them all back to their masters. Now he didn't have to convince every dog to stay with him in the wild. Didn't have to convince every part of *himself* to stay.

Pumpkin slouched down where she sat, curling up like a tiny sad cloud in the dirt.

"What about Zeus?" Oscar barked.

Shep turned to the pup, who stood in front of the boxer. Zeus was nearly invisible beside the tunnel's entrance.

"He can't be a part of my pack," Shep growled.

"What pack?" snarled Zeus. "These dogs all want to go home to their nice beds and dry kibble."

"Whatever we are, I don't want you to be a part of it," Shep grumbled back.

Oscar hopped onto a large rock so that he was nearly snout-to-snout with Shep. "Pumpkin is Zeus's and my best shot at getting home, too. You can't drive us away when she could help us get back to our families."

"I'm not driving you away, Oscar," Shep said.

"I'm not going to leave Zeus," the pup barked. "He's only got three good legs. How will he get food? He'll never survive without help. And if you and the others won't help him, then I guess it's left to me."

Both Zeus and Shep had the same expression of disbelief on their muzzles.

"I don't need help to survive," growled Zeus.

"He'll kill you for kibble, Oscar," Shep snarled at the same time.

"Yes, you do need help," barked Oscar, "and no, he won't kill me. He could've killed me at any point tonight and he didn't." He looked at Zeus and grinned. "He's changed. He did bad, but now he wants to do good."

Zeus raised his jowl. Only for a heartbeat, but Shep saw it — that look of disgust. He'd seen it on his friend's muzzle many times before. Zeus didn't agree with a woof the pup barked. He hadn't changed a hair in his coat.

"You can believe what you want," Shep woofed. "But that dog there is a killer. You can follow his scent, but he's only leading you to slaughter."

Oscar's tail sank and his ears flapped against his muzzle. "Well, then, I guess this is good-bye." The pup hopped off the rock and loped to Zeus's flank.

Shep couldn't let the fur-brained pup just toss himself to the Black Dog like that. Not when Shep knew what Zeus would do to him.

"Oscar," he barked. "Don't go." He forced the barks through his gritted teeth. "You're right," he continued. "Pumpkin could be a way for you both to get home."

Zeus stood, his ears forward. An unsettling grin appeared on his jowls.

"But Zeus can't sleep with us," Shep snapped. "He has to keep at least fifteen stretches away, and I want him on the sunset side of the tunnel. You can stay here or with him, but those are my rules."

Oscar leapt at Shep's snout, tail in full swing. "Oh, Shep! You're just the greatest! And you won't regret this! Zeus will be a model dog, I promise."

Shep licked the pup. "I'm not holding my breath," he woofed.

"He's changed," yipped Oscar. "I can smell it." He turned to Zeus. "Come on!" Then he raced into the dark, on the sunset side of the tunnel.

Zeus squinted at Shep like he was about to woof something. But the big dog just snorted and followed Oscar into the shadows.

Shep sniffed deeply, catching their scents and locating them in the palette of odors swirling through the swamp. He noted where each of the other dogs slept, and what their exact smells were so he could note any nuance of change in their scents — even when sleeping, a dog would have a heartbeat of reaction time before being killed, and that's all Shep would need to know Zeus was on the prowl. If he had to keep the boxer nearby to keep him from killing Oscar, so be it, but he wouldn't let Zeus catch him unawares ever again.

Shep curled himself in the middle of the clearing. He rested his long muzzle on his paws, pointed toward where Oscar and Zeus had disappeared, and closed his eyes. He did not sleep. His ears constantly twitched, marking every movement in the wood, and his nostrils fluttered, catching every scent that blew by.

CHAPTER 5
DENWARD BOUND

Shep smelled Callie's approach. The tails of dawn had just begun to wag in the sky behind Shep — their dim light outlined the rim of the tunnel. Before him, the sky was still deep blue and a few fires of the Great Wolf's coat glittered along the tree line.

"You're up early," he woofed.

"I figured you hadn't slept," Callie replied. She sat beside Shep's snout. "I remember what that was like — no rest for the alpha."

"You've gotten more sleep while trapped in that cage?" Shep shifted his muzzle to the other side of his paws, away from Callie.

"What else could I do?" she woofed. She licked one front dewclaw and rubbed it over her short muzzle. "It was loud in that building and the lights were always on, but I was so tired I could have slept in the middle of the street with Cars whizzing over my back."

Shep decided to dig straight into the idea he'd been chewing on all night. "I want to rebuild the pack," he barked. "Now that you and I are back together, we have a real chance at surviving."

Callie placed her paw on the ground and looked at Shep. She planted a light lick on his wet nose. "I can't," she woofed. "I'm sorry, Shep, but I want to go home. I want to be with my family."

Shep pushed himself to sitting. "But why?" he yipped. "It was you who wanted to escape your den back on that grate, before the storm."

Callie grinned. "A lot's happened since we met on that grate. For starters, I nearly died."

Shep panted lightly. "Nearly," he snuffled. "But we've learned so much. I think we could really make it, especially with the humans coming back. There'll be more food to scavenge —"

"Shep," Callie yipped softly. "You're not hearing me. I don't want to rebuild the pack. I want to return to my girl."

"I thought we were partners," Shep grumbled. "I thought you wanted to lead the dogs."

"I did," she woofed. "But that was when we didn't know where our humans were, when all we had were our fellow dogs to rely on. Now our humans are here — they never left! And we can find them. Don't you smell how different the situation is?"

Shep licked his jowls and scanned the surrounding scents — Zeus was still in his pile of leaves with Oscar; every other dog snored on. "How is the situation different?" he barked. "Pumpkin doesn't know where she is, let alone how to get to this 'shelter.' And what if the place was destroyed in the storm? What if our families are —" He stopped himself, knowing he'd gone too far.

Callie stared at him, frightened by what he'd almost said. "I won't believe such a thing until I've smelled it myself." She shivered. "I have to believe that, with or without Pumpkin, we will find our families. The humans are here. The city is no longer abandoned." Callie sniffed the air. "I can smell them, all around. Even if we just go back to our dens, I'm sure our families will return for us."

"I don't want to go back." Shep felt ashamed barking the woofs out loud. "I want to be free."

Callie smiled a gentle smile and rubbed her muzzle against his shoulder. "Wearing a collar doesn't mean you're not free," she said.

"You won't be able to see me whenever you want," Shep grunted. "Or eat what you want. Or chase squirrels through the street."

"True," woofed Callie. "But I won't starve, or eat a poisonous plant trying not to starve, or lose fur over whether I made the right decision by letting a black Lab den with a Boston terrier. I'll be well fed and in an air-conditioned den with a soft bed, just for me. And I'll run around in a safe Park without worrying about whether a pack of wild dogs is going to tear my ear off."

"There will always be a leash holding you back."

"No matter where you go, Shep," Callie snuffled, "there's always something holding on to you, whether it's a leash or a pack or your stomach." She waved her snout at the trees, standing black against the lightening sky. "Life isn't about freedom; it's about choosing what you want to be free *from*. I want to be free from worry. This last moon-cycle, I've worried enough for one lifetime."

Shep closed his eyes. Callie was set on her track — he'd failed to convince her to stay. The only question was whether he should take off now and leave the dogs to find their way home alone, or stand by his pack and lead them to safety. Why did he even bother asking the question? There was no other choice but to lead his friends home. *It's what an alpha does.*

"If it's what you want," he woofed, "I'll take you home. But I'm staying free."

A frown clouded Callie's muzzle for a heartbeat, but then she licked his nose. "Thank you," she yipped.

Pumpkin woke with a scream. "GET IT OFF ME! GET IT OFF ME!" She bounded in small circles, kicking and scratching and biting her fur.

"What?" barked Shep. "What happened?" He hadn't smelled or heard Zeus prowling and couldn't see anything near her.

"A fly!" Pumpkin shrieked. "A horrible, buzzing, nasty, disease-ridden, spiny-haired ball of evil with wings!"

Shep cocked his head. "You're tearing your fur out over a *fly*?"

Pumpkin stopped bouncing and panted, nervously twitching every few heartbeats. "They're evil, I tell you. Pure evil." Then she shook herself from nose to tail, licked her jowls, and smiled. "I know how we can find the shelter!" Just like that, it was as if Shep were barking with a different dog. "I had this dream," she yipped to Shep and Callie, who'd joined Shep in staring at the white dog like she'd morphed into an iguana.

"I was back home," Pumpkin continued, "sleeping in my favorite bed by the window, looking down at the beach." She looked at each of them with a huge smile on her snout, her tiny tail waving.

"And?" woofed Callie encouragingly.

"And what?" barked Pumpkin, head tilted.

"How does this dream help us at all?" grumbled Shep.

"The *beach*, silly fur!" yapped Pumpkin. She slapped her paws on the dirt. "If we go to the beach, we can find my den!"

Shep sank into a sit and scratched his scruff. "We're nowhere near the beach," he grunted. "And even if we got to the beach, how would you know where your den is? The beach is a huge, long strip of sand, and the only scents I ever smelled there were salt and rotting weeds."

"I'd know *my* beach anywhere," Pumpkin woofed with her snout raised, like a tiny, white version of Ginny.

"Any other ideas?" Shep woofed to Callie.

"No," she replied, "but I think Pumpkin might be onto something."

Pumpkin sprang to her paws, vibrating with excitement. "Yes! I am!" She waved her tail and waited for Callie to continue.

Callie looked at the fluffy girldog as if even *she* found Pumpkin's exuberance disturbing. "What I mean is that traveling on the beach, rather than the streets, back to our dens would mean that we would run into fewer humans. It might be safer."

"Yes!" yipped Pumpkin. "It would be supersafe!"

"There are always humans on the beach," grumbled Shep. "And there are no buildings to hide in or scavenge for food."

"I don't think the humans have returned to the city to sunbathe," barked Callie. "I think they have a few other things nibbling at them besides how brown their skin is."

"Is that what all those people were doing?" woofed Shep. "They sleep on the sand to turn brown?"

"My mistress sleeps on the sand all the time," yipped Pumpkin. "I love the sand!"

"And there are buildings alongside the beach," woofed Callie. "Maybe there will be food inside those dens."

"Yes!" barked Pumpkin. "My den is next to the beach!"

Shep had that feeling again, of wanting to drop a paw on the little white yapper and plant her in the dirt like a palm tree. *That's not how an alpha should be thinking,* he reminded himself and pressed his paws more firmly onto the ground.

"If that's what you think is best," he woofed to Callie, "I'm willing to go along with your plan."

The other dogs had woken at the sound of Pumpkin's excited barks. They now crowded around the three of them.

Shep turned his attention to Pumpkin, who bounced on her paws. "So, how do we get to your beach?" he barked as calmly as possible.

Pumpkin furrowed her fluffy brow and nibbled a jowl, putting on a bit of a show for her audience. "Well, the sun rises over the beach, so we should walk toward sunrise until we hit the ocean. Then we'll be at the beach!"

"We're thousands of stretches from the ocean," Zeus growled, padding into the clearing. "How does the yapper suppose we're going to get from here all the way to the beach without getting caught by the dog catchers?" He limped over the dribble of water streaming out of the tunnel and sat near the scrubby bushes that grew under the trees.

Shep's hackles rose, as did every other dog's — except Pumpkin's; she seemed oblivious to Zeus's menace.

"That's no problem!" she yipped. "There aren't that many people working to catch dogs — I only saw a couple in the kennel. The night they brought in Callie and the other dogs you were with, the humans had been yapping about a 'nest of dogs,' how they had to 'break up the nest,' so I think maybe whoever caught you was a special group organized to catch your pack. Most of the people here are trying to help clean up the mess that the storm left."

Rufus snorted a nasty little snort, always happy to contribute some tail-dragger comment. "I'd bet my snout that any human would call the dog catchers the heartbeat they spotted us, whether they were working with them or not."

Pumpkin — immune even to Rufus's nastiness — wagged her tail and continued yapping happily. "Not if you're superfriendly, they won't!"

"I agree with the young ladydog," yipped Ginny. "I think we've been taking the wrong track with all this sneaking about. Humans love dogs. If we just show a sniff of poise and reflect an open countenance, they will do anything for us."

"I have no idea what the poofy yapper just said, but I don't like the smell of it," grumbled Zeus.

"She said we have to act nice and approachable,"

Callie barked. "A task it's not clear you can handle." She growled softly on her last woofs.

Zeus sneered, but kept quiet.

Well, that is a change, Shep noted. *Time was, he'd have bitten her snout off for that. . . .*

Pumpkin reared in front of Zeus, planted her paws on his chest, and began sniffing his jowls and turning her head from side to side. "Oh, I think that we can make him look friendly," she woofed, unaware that she was a heartbeat away from getting swiped with a fang.

Zeus, however, kept his cool. He grimaced at the yapper's shiny black nose as it wuffled in his ear, but let her finish her analysis of his "countenance" . . . whatever that was.

Ginny watched Pumpkin's brave investigation of Zeus with a look of shock but then paraded closer to the boxer herself and gave him a perfunctory sniff. "Yes," she yipped. "I think that Pumpkin and I can make you all seem like the friendliest bunch of dogs this side of the swamplands." She gave a nod of her snout and a wave of her tail.

Dover looked at Shep, eyebrows raised. Shep had no idea how Pumpkin thought she could turn Zeus into a friendly dog, but, Great Wolf, he was happy to let her try.

CHAPTER 6
LESSONS ON FRIENDLINESS AND APPROACHABILITY

Rufus was adamant about finding some kibble before any dog attempted to transform Zeus into a friendly dog. "We'll all have starved to death before she gives up on this fuzz-headed plan," he grumbled.

"No need to get growly," Callie barked. "But I agree with Rufus. My tummy's rumbling!"

Shep wagged his tail. "Who's up for some hunting?" he woofed. He glanced at Callie and saw the excitement flash across her muzzle.

"First dog to catch a squirrel gets first choice of kibble!" Callie howled. She sprang into the brush and began snuffling through the leaves.

Shep dove after her. He took a deep breath, scented all possible prey, and dashed after a squirrel hidden in a

72

tussock of grass. Pure joy pulsed through him like life-blood. How could he give this up? Hunting felt as necessary to his life now as breathing. Callie was wrong — life on a leash could never make him this happy. He watched Callie tear after a fleeing bird and saw the smile on her jowls. He knew she felt that same spark running under her fur. *Give her time*, he thought. *Maybe after a sun or two out of her cage, she'll remember how great pack life can be.*

Callie downed two squirrels, Dover nabbed a rat, and Shep caught a rabbit, which meant there was enough meat for all. Fuzz offered to share some of the grasshoppers he'd caught, but no dog accepted the invitation.

"No need to choke down bugs — *snort* — when there's meat in the bowl!" Daisy yipped, licking her jowls.

Oscar stood near her, struggling to tear the leg off the rabbit. He jammed his little paws into the hide, tugged, and fell flat on his tail. Shep wondered if this was one of those let-the-pup-figure-it-out-himself situations. Before he came to a decision, Daisy strutted up to Oscar and shoved him aside.

"I can do it!" yipped Oscar as Daisy wrenched the bones apart.

"Just shut your snout," Daisy growled. She spat the meat at his paws.

Oscar looked at the rabbit hock. "You didn't have to help me."

Daisy's ears and tail relaxed, like she was going to maybe give the poor pup a lick, but then she reasserted her tough stance. "I couldn't — *snort* — let you ruin the whole rabbit with your scratching." She turned back to her meal.

"Thank you," Oscar snuffled.

Daisy didn't give him so much as a snort, but Shep smelled that she was straining every muscle in her rump to keep from wagging her tail.

After catching a slurp of water in the stream, the small pack assembled in the clearing for Pumpkin's Lessons on Friendliness and Approachability, as Ginny had labeled them.

"It's all about the tail," Pumpkin began. She held hers straight up like a tree trunk.

"Some of us are tail deficient," barked Zeus flatly. He nodded toward his rump, where his stub of a tail lay.

Pumpkin didn't let his tone faze her. "It doesn't matter how big your tail is, so long as it's wagging!" She gave her tail a swish, and its long hairs waved behind it. "Any human is going to feel better about a dog if its tail is wagging, so the first rule is: See a human, wag your tail."

"What-if-it's-a-dog-catcher-human-should-I-still-wag-my-tail?" Snoop was paying unusually close attention to Pumpkin's lecture.

"Yes!" she woofed.

"No," barked Shep at the same time.

Pumpkin gave Shep a head tilt. "Aren't *I* in charge of these lessons?" she yapped.

Shep barely controlled a growl. "You may be in charge of teaching this pack how to look cute, but I'm still in charge of every dog's safety." He scanned the dogs' muzzles to make sure they understood, ending on Snoop's narrow snout. Snoop licked his jowls, looked sheepishly at the dirt, then began to nibble an itch on his leg.

Shep continued, "You see a dog catcher, you run. Don't waste time wiggling your rump."

"I disagree," yipped Callie. "How are we going to know who's a dog catcher, anyway? All the people I saw at the kennel were dressed like regular people. As Pumpkin woofed, the team that invaded the boat was a special group. I say we treat all humans as friends until they show us different."

The other dogs wagged their tails in agreement. Zeus snickered.

Shep straightened his stance, lifted his muzzle, and replied in his most important-sounding bark. "You're not disagreeing with me, Callie," he woofed. "I said the same thing — you can wag your tail at any regular human, but don't waste time if you see a man in green. If the dog catcher is dressed like a regular human, they're probably not going to shoot you with a dart."

The pack seemed confused, like they weren't quite sure why there was so much barking on this issue of tail wagging. But they didn't think about things the way an alpha had to. They had the luxury of just living a regular life. Shep had to constantly be on his guard for any divisions in the ranks, for any cracks in his authority. As Callie had once warned him, the last thing the pack needed was a power struggle.

Callie cocked her head at Shep, as if about to argue, but then sat down. "You're right, Shep," she woofed. "I should have stated that differently. I just want to make sure there are no unfortunate mistakes, like what happened at the kennel." She emphasized her last woofs.

"What happened at the kennel?" asked Boji, concerned.

"Noth —" Shep began, but Pumpkin was already barking.

"Shep attacked this nice lady who worked in the medical building."

The other dogs looked at Shep as if he'd attacked their own families.

"You *attacked* a human?" snuffled Ginny with a tremulous bark.

Even Dover seemed flustered by this revelation. For the first time, he looked at Shep like he wasn't sure of his character, like Shep was a bad dog.

"He didn't 'attack her,' attack her," barked Callie, interrupting the anxious silence. "He pushed her and she fell over a table. The woman was trying to catch him. Shep was only trying to help me escape." She sat next to Shep and licked his snout. "He feels really bad about it," she added.

Shep caught her scent. "Yes," he woofed. Then he repeated it in a more assured bark. "Yes, I feel terrible about pushing the woman." And he realized, in barking it, that all these heartbeats later, he still felt itchy under his fur. It was as if in pushing a human, he'd violated nature and his own body was delivering the punishment.

The dogs smelled a bit friendlier toward Shep, though Ginny still stuck her snout slightly in the air when she looked at him.

Pumpkin shook herself to regain the pack's attention. "I think we can use this," she yipped. "See, Shep thought that the only way to get away from the nice lady was to attack her, but he had loads of other options. For one, he could have wagged his tail, like I've been barking. If he had played along, like he was going to do whatever she wanted, the heartbeat her back was turned, he could have run. No one's fur would have gotten ruffled! But this requires changing your whole view of things. It's not just about wagging your tail, it's about *meaning* it.

"Humans are kind of thick when it comes to dogs. They see a cute muzzle and big eyes and get all mushy about the brain and start cooing and sticking their hands out. All you need to do is answer this natural tendency to go mushy-brained by wagging your tail in a friendly, assertive manner — up high, big swishes from side to side."

"What if you don't have a cute muzzle?" grunted Zeus. "Or a tail?"

Pumpkin sighed and flicked her ears. "Well, you're just going to have to work harder," she woofed. "Admittedly, for cute dogs like Ginny and me, and puppies like Oscar, this is a piece of jerky. Heck, most humans even go gaga for wrinkled-up, crazy muzzles like Daisy's."

"I'm standing — *snort* — right here!" Daisy growled.

"What are you getting your tail in a knot about?" Pumpkin yipped. "I'm saying people think you're cute!"

She swatted a paw at Daisy with a little flourish of her head. Daisy was so bewildered she shut her jowls and smiled nervously.

Pumpkin strutted up to Zeus. "With you, I think the best tactic is to make yourself smaller."

"I don't get smaller." Zeus met her gaze with a look of pure disgust.

"Oh, quit your growling, you big pile of hair! You can too get smaller. You could do a front-paw slap and *poof*!" Pumpkin flopped down onto her chest, front paws out in front of her. "You look shorter."

"My front paw's in a cast," Zeus grunted.

Pumpkin sighed. "Dog, you really are a tail dragger!" she yipped. "Work with me, will you!" She leapt at his jowl and planted a lick on his snout. Zeus's eyes nearly bugged out of his head.

Pumpkin wagged her tail and cocked her muzzle. "I think maybe a full lie-down with stub-tail wag and goo-goo eyes will be just the thing for you."

"Goo-goo eyes?" Zeus grumbled incredulously.

"Like this," yipped Pumpkin. She flounced onto her belly, then looked up at the treetops and sucked her jowls down. Her eyes bulged to gigantic beads of black. She fluttered her eyelids. "The fluttering says, 'Don't you love me?' but I think you, Zeus, should go for 'Play with me!'" She grinned with her jowls and panted slightly, straining her eyes open wide and whipping her tail back and forth. Then she gave a few light barks. Suddenly, as if a switch were turned off, she stood and shook her fur.

"Okay, let's see you do it," she yipped, sitting down and considering Zeus with a steady gaze.

Zeus looked nervously at Shep, but Shep wasn't going to let Zeus out of this. *You want to pretend to be a different, not-evil dog, pretend away....*

"Just lie down?" Zeus woofed.

"Don't forget the goo-goo eyes," yapped Rufus in a snide bark.

Zeus growled at the squaredog, which shut Rufus's snout, but lay down like Pumpkin had asked. He winced as he settled his hurt paw, then forced his jowls into a smile and panted. He wiggled his stumpy tail and bugged his eyes as far out of his skull as he could manage. The effect was too horrible to bear.

"He looks worse than a monster," moaned Ginny.

"He *is* a monster," growled Boji, who glared at Zeus from the shadows.

"Are-those-goo-goo-eyes-because-if-so-I-think-they-are-scary-and-maybe-also-terrifying-and-yes-please-make-him-stop," Snoop yammered.

Pumpkin sniffed disapprovingly. "I do agree," she yipped. "This isn't working for you." She cocked her head. "Really, you have to stop."

Zeus let his eyelids drop and pushed himself back up to sitting. "So you're going to leave me to the dog catchers?" he grumbled. "I'm too nasty even to fake out a human?"

"No, no," yipped Pumpkin cheerfully. "I just had you doing the wrong thing. Let's play up the limp."

Pumpkin worked with each dog this way, helping them find the best paw to put forward if they ran into a human. She turned to Shep last.

"You," she woofed, considering him like a kibble in a bowl. "You're going to be the hardest to sell."

"Me?" woofed Shep, tilting his head. "I'm a perfect gentleman when it comes to humans."

Pumpkin grimaced. Rufus snorted. Even Callie looked less than convinced.

"Really," Shep woofed. "Except for that one time, I have a perfectly good relationship with humans." He couldn't believe these dogs all thought he was going to be a tougher sell than Zeus.

"Look," Pumpkin yipped, shrugging. "I'm not going to gravy-coat this for you — German shepherds are used by humans to attack other humans, so people are wary of your kind."

"Wary? What are you saying, people don't like me?" Shep had never had a problem with people liking him . . . well, that wasn't exactly true. His boy liked him, and his family, but he'd never really concerned himself with how other people felt about him. Now that he thought about it, other people generally leaned away from him or crossed the street. It had never bothered him — what did he care about other people? — but Pumpkin had her nose on a scent: It might take some work to convince a stranger that he was friendly.

"Okay," Shep woofed, sitting. "Maybe I do look a little . . . scary. What can I do?"

Oscar sat down beside Shep. "I don't think you look scary," he woofed, smiling up at Shep.

Shep panted gently. "Thanks," he woofed. "But I'm trying to convince a nervous human that I'm not a threat, and I happen to know that I *am* a threat. Apparently, they know it, too."

All the dogs, even Zeus, woofed ideas for how to make Shep more friendly looking. "Maybe he could pretend to have a limp?" "Maybe we could give him a real limp?" "Maybe he could slap the ground, like he wanted to play?" "Maybe have him carry a stick around?" "More tail wagging?" "Less panting?" "Friendlier eyes?" "Floppier ears?" But every posture or prop or muzzle tic was met with disapproval by the other dogs.

"Not even Lassie herself could help you look appealing, Shep," Ginny yapped finally. She dropped into a sit in the moss by the stream.

Fuzz sat beside Shep. "Fuzz watch for person," the cat hissed. "Keep Shep-dog from make scary-snout at wrong heartbeat."

"What if Shep is just himself?" yipped Oscar. He hopped onto a rock and nodded his snout at Shep. "I mean, all dogs don't have to be cute, right? Maybe Shep is just, well, Shep. I think he looks honorable and proud and like he'd face a whole pack of wild dogs to save you, and that's good, too, right? Even if it's not particularly cute." Oscar waved his tail, and the pack wagged their tails in agreement.

Callie smiled. "I think, Oscar, that is *exactly* right."

CHAPTER 7
THE LEGEND OF LASSIE

Shep announced that the pack would wait until dark before setting out for the shelter.

"Can't we just walk to the edge of the Park?" whined Pumpkin. "No one will see us in the Park."

"I don't know that," Shep woofed. "Who knows if there are people in here? There could be dog catchers looking for you and Callie right this heartbeat. No, we wait until night. Better safe than captured."

Shep was stalling — he wasn't ready to let his friends leave. If the other dogs smelled this, they kept it to themselves. They didn't argue with his order. Even Callie kept whatever thoughts she had to herself.

Pumpkin sulked in the corner of the clearing under a scrubby bush, then sprang up yelping about the horrible insect that buzzed by her ear. Zeus retreated to his nest of leaves near the tunnel and Oscar followed him, yapping at Zeus about whether he needed help with his paw or a drink or something to eat.

Shep curled up on the bank of the stream. He couldn't shake the dread that covered him like a coat of mud. He didn't want to take the pack to the shelter. Even if he didn't go home, what was he going to do, run around the city alone? How would he form a new pack? In truth, he didn't want a new pack — he wanted his friends to stay with him, to *want* to stay with him. He wanted things to go back to how they used to be.

Pumpkin sighed with a dramatic flourish of her tail. "There's nothing to *do* until sunset," she whined.

Snoop pawed a dead branch. "Want-to-play-Big-Stick-huh-please?" he yipped.

Pumpkin trotted toward Snoop, tail wagging. "I want to play! But I'm too small for Big Stick. Does any dog have a Ball?"

Daisy snorted. "Where would one of us have gotten a Ball?"

The white girldog slumped into a sit. "Fine, then I'll just sit here and watch my fur grow."

Rufus growled from his nest under a bush. "You're not making the heartbeats pass any faster by whining."

Ginny shook herself, rustling the dead leaves around her. "How about I tell you a story?" she yipped.

"Oh, yes!" barked Pumpkin. "I would love a story! What's a story?" She waved her tail and smiled at the dogs.

"It's something Shep dug up," woofed Ginny.

"I didn't dig up anything," Shep snuffled. "All I did was woof to Callie what an old timer had snuffled to me when I was a frightened pup. You and Oscar took that stick and ran with it."

"And look at all the trouble that — *snort* — caused," grumbled Daisy.

"How could some old timer's woofs cause trouble?" yipped Pumpkin.

"Trouble? Pish posh," snapped Ginny. "Oscar's and my stories made a whole pack of abandoned pets feel safe in this storm-wrecked world. Whatever else happened wasn't the stories' fault." She looked sternly toward where Oscar hid behind the tunnel wall.

"These story-things sound very powerful," woofed Pumpkin in a hushed bark. "Do they bite?"

"In a matter of barking," Ginny answered, a smile on her jowls, "I guess they do. This one is about a dog who's woofed to me all my life."

Many cycles ago, there was a dog named Lassie, and she was loyal and kind to other dogs. One sun, she caught a strange scent. Worried that this scent might be from a threat to her pack, she followed it through the woods. It led her out of her pack's territory, far from her den, through strange waters and thick leaves. She began to worry that she'd gone too far following this new smell, but she also felt that having come so far she could not turn back until she found its source.

Night fell over the forest. Lassie looked up at the Great Wolf's glittering coat and asked him for guidance. As if answering her howl, one of the furs in his coat blazed for several heartbeats. Lassie thanked the Great Wolf and dashed toward where the fire had burned in the night.

The fire led her to a small, hairless animal curled in the grass. Lassie licked the thing and it stirred. She ducked away from the animal but then remembered that the Great Wolf had led her there so this animal must not be dangerous.

The hairless animal stretched, its gangly limbs protruding from its body like branches from a tree.

"What are you?" woofed Lassie.

The hairless creature started. But Lassie wagged her tail, and the creature calmed. It extended its limb, which had a sort of paw with long toes stuck on its end. Lassie raised her paw, and the creature wrapped its long toes around her pads.

They both were shocked at the spark that ran through their lifeblood at the touch of their paws. It was as if Lassie had bathed in sunlight; she felt her fur glow. The creature's eyes sparkled. Its smooth cheeks warmed to a rosy pink and its lips curled into a wide smile.

The creature opened its mouth. "You are good," the creature said. "I am a boy. What are you?"

Lassie told the boy that she was a dog. She told him that there were many like her, and about how the Great Wolf had taught her pack to live in peace.

The boy shook his head. "Humans are not happy the way you dogs are. We fight and struggle and live in fear."

"That sounds terrible," woofed Lassie.

The boy and Lassie sat together, him with his arm around her neck and she with her head against his shoulder, and the warm glow radiated through them.

In the morning, the boy stroked Lassie's fur. He had an idea. "Lassie, you should come to my den and tell the humans about the Great Wolf. Maybe then we can learn to live in peace like the dogs."

Lassie agreed, and the boy began to lead her back to his den.

As they walked, the scent of their happiness — that warm glow of connection — wafted throughout the forest. It drifted up to the Great Wolf, and he smiled; it drifted down to the Black Dog, and he scowled.

"What new joy has the Great Wolf delivered?" he snarled. For the Black Dog hated anything favored by the Great Wolf.

The Black Dog skulked up from the depths, winding his way through the shadows, and soon caught up with Lassie and the boy. He saw the golden glow shining around them and was disgusted.

"No dog should be so happy," he growled.

The boy introduced Lassie to his people and explained what Lassie had told him. "Lassie and the Great Wolf could teach us to live in peace," the boy said.

These words raised hackles along the Black Dog's bony spine. He could never allow the Great Wolf's influence to spread so far. He had to distract Lassie before she had a chance to speak.

The Black Dog turned himself into a pup and began whimpering and crying. Lassie heard the pup's cries and told the boy that she had to see what was the matter. The boy begged her not to go, but Lassie could not ignore a dog in need.

"I will go with you," said the boy, and the two ran off together.

When they arrived at the thicket where the pup lay crying, the boy knelt beside the small dog.

"Don't cry," the boy said. "My touch will make you feel better."

He laid his hand on the bristly coat, and the Black Dog revealed his true form.

"Your touch will never be felt by another dog," the Black Dog snarled.

A hole opened beneath him and sucked both the Black Dog and the boy down into the earth.

Lassie shrieked with terror. She ran back to the human den for help. She told the boy's kin about the Black Dog's treachery and begged them to help her save the boy. But the humans did not listen. They yelled at Lassie and blamed her for the boy's disappearance. They struck her, called her bad, and demanded that she leave all the clan's boys and girls alone.

But Lassie could not abandon her boy. Even if his kin would not help her, even if they hated and feared all dogs, she could not leave him prey to the wrath of the Black Dog.

Lassie ran back to the hole and crept down into it. She followed the Black Dog's trail deep under the earth until she found him in his cave. The boy lay limp in his jowls.

"Leave us, or I will kill this boy," the Black Dog barked.

"You must kill me first," Lassie howled fiercely. "I will never leave my boy." She dove at the Black Dog's jaws and tore the boy from his grasp.

Their battle shook the roots of the earth. Dogs heard Lassie's cries and ran to aid their packmate. The humans heard the boy yell for Lassie's help and knew that they had misjudged the dog. They, too, raced to save their boy. But all were too late. When the dogs and humans arrived, they found poor Lassie slumped over her boy and the boy dead in her paws. The Black Dog disappeared in a foul mist. All that remained of his evil was a nasty pant that echoed throughout the cave.

The Great Wolf shone into this darkest cavern and his misery rained down as a soft, silver light. "What has happened to my Lassie?" he howled. "You humans did not believe her barks, yet she woofed the truth."

The Great Wolf wrapped his fiery paws around Lassie's fallen form and raised her up into the sky. But Lassie's spirit cried out, "Please, bring my boy with me!"

The Great Wolf then took up the boy, too, so that he and Lassie could sparkle as one golden fire in the sky.

The humans and dogs looked at one another. In their sadness, they came together, and in coming together, they felt that golden glow that Lassie and the boy had found.

But the Great Wolf punished humans for their folly and took away their ability to understand dogs. And so we muddle along, happy together, but unable to fully express our devotion as Lassie and her boy once could.

The pack was silent after Ginny finished her story, they were so absorbed in the tale. Even Shep wished to live in that world — he could almost believe in the Great Wolf again the way Ginny woofed it.

"Wow," yipped Pumpkin. "Where can I get more stories like that?"

Ginny beamed, tail waving at the compliments of every dog. "Well, how did you meet your family? There might be a story there."

"My girl came to where I was born and picked me out of the whole litter of pups to be her superstar show dog," barked Pumpkin, preening as she pranced in the dirt.

"I was the pup of two show dogs," woofed Ginny. "But you all could probably tell that from my coat." She flicked her tail, sending its long hairs sailing over the dust. "Alas, that's not much of a story. What about the rest of you?"

Dover, Boji, and Rufus had all been picked from their litters like Ginny and Pumpkin. Daisy and Oscar both came from the store.

"I was rescued from a shelter as a puppy," Callie barked when asked where she came from. "I was born there to a shelter dog."

"Did you have any littermates?" asked Pumpkin. "Maybe that could also be a story? 'A Pup and Her Littermates.'"

"I don't remember," snuffled Callie, tail low.

"My first family gave me away when they had a baby," Zeus growled from the shadows. Apparently, the story had lured him to the edges of the pack. "They pretended to love me until they found something better. Turn that into a story."

"That's a terrible story," yipped Pumpkin. "Can a story be terrible?" She cocked her head in Ginny's direction.

"Not any story I want to hear," she groaned.

"I don't give a ripped toy if his story is terrible," grumbled Rufus. "It doesn't excuse anything he did. He's still a bad dog, no matter what happened to him."

Shep didn't disagree with Rufus — just because Zeus's first family had abandoned him didn't make up for the fact that Zeus had murdered dogs, their friends. But still, Shep hadn't known that about his friend — his ex-friend. Zeus had always seemed a little distant, a little afraid of getting too close, like it was fine to play in the

Park together, but forget anything else. Not that with collars around their necks, they could have done more. But he wondered if maybe they had barked about it, back when they had been friends in the Park, would Zeus have run off and joined the wild pack? Could things have been different if they had been better friends?

Shep wondered how well he knew any of these dogs. For all the suns they'd spent together, they'd had precious few heartbeats to just woof about themselves. Shep wanted to know his pack better, and now that chance was slipping away. All so that these dogs could return to their collars, to the families that left them behind. *Now that's an idea. . . .*

"I've got a story for you," Shep woofed. "Once there was a pup who was born in the fight kennel. He grew up and escaped the fight cage only to find himself caught in a harsh world run by wild dogs. He thought he was saved when he was taken in by his boy, but then his boy abandoned him to be eaten by a storm."

He looked at his packmates to see if they'd caught his scent; they looked at him with stricken muzzles, tails low and still.

He continued, "But this story has a happy ending. That dog met an amazing girldog and they rescued other dogs left alone in the storm by their families. She helped him to smell that dogs are meant to live as a pack, not alone in human dens."

He scanned the snouts of his friends. "Are you sure you want to go home to the humans who abandoned you?" he barked. "Why don't we all stay here? There's lots of prey to hunt in the Park. We dogs can rely on each other!" He smiled and panted and waved his tail.

No tail answered his wag.

Callie loped to Shep's side. She winced a small, tight smile. "I'm sorry, Shep," she woofed. "But we want to go home." She licked his nose. "Your boy loves you. I'm certain that if he could have taken you with him, he would have."

All the dogs pressed closer to Shep and Callie, as if trying to take comfort from her woofs. They smelled scared and sad — Shep hadn't made them want to stay with him; he'd made them think their families hated them. What kind of alpha did a thing like that?

Pumpkin cocked her muzzle. "You all seem so, how can I bark this, kind of desperate? Crazy?" she yipped. "I mean, your humans love you. It's like in Ginny's story-thing — humans and dogs need each other. Once we get to the shelter, you'll see!"

"Easy for you to woof," Zeus snapped. "Your mistress never left you. You never had to fight for your life on the streets."

"True," woofed Pumpkin. "But that's all over now. You're almost home."

"There's a lot of city between us and home," Dover barked, shaking himself. He turned to Shep and with a stern gaze woofed, "The sun's setting."

Shep licked his jowls. He'd made his pitch as best he could; he didn't want to upset his pack any further. If no dog wanted to stay with him, he'd have to form a new pack. But he'd promised Callie he'd get her home, and he would not break a promise to her.

"Let's get into formation," he howled.

CHAPTER 8
STREETWISE

Shep gave the dogs a few heartbeats to slurp some water and otherwise get ready to hit the trail.

Oscar crept up to Shep's flank, trembling. "Did my family leave me because they saw I was a bad dog?" he whimpered. "Do you think they knew?"

Shep could not have felt like a bigger pile of scat.

He lay down beside the pup and let his ears flap loose. "No, Oscar," he snuffled. "I think your family loves you. Listen to Callie's woofs. Just believe that they love you."

"You don't." Oscar looked at his paws.

"I want to believe," he answered truthfully. He wished he could believe that his boy loved him, that the Great

Wolf still watched over him, that his pack still saw him as an alpha — he desperately wanted back his faith in *everything*.

Oscar snuggled against Shep's fur. "Do you think the pack will ever forgive me?" he yipped. "Can I ever be a good dog again?"

Shep recalled asking Callie the same thing so many suns ago, after he told her about what happened to YipYowl. "Once, pup, I did something bad — I was scared and angry and I did something I couldn't forgive myself for. Callie told me that it wasn't about whether I was a good dog or a bad dog. She said I just had to keep *trying* to be a good dog."

"Like the Great Wolf," Oscar yipped.

Shep licked the pup's head. "Yeah," he woofed. "Just like the Great Wolf."

Daisy came over to where they stood. "Is the pup bothering you?" she growled.

Oscar glanced up at Daisy's muzzle. Her wrinkles had twisted into an angry scowl. The pup yelped and slunk away toward his and Zeus's nest.

"You shouldn't be so hard on him," Shep woofed.

"If I'd been harder on him," Daisy grumbled, "maybe he wouldn't have turned out to be such a fur-brain."

"You do recall that he's a part of your family?" Shep yipped. "If you go home, you're going with him."

Daisy waved her tail. "Don't — *snort* — remind me." She licked her nose. "If I had any faith in your planning skills, Alpha, I'd stay with you." She strutted off toward the stream, yapping at Boji about scent trails.

As she left, Fuzz crept out of the shadows, his snout stuffed with dead insects. He spat them into the dirt at Shep's paws.

"While Shep-dog give pack sad-tail, Fuzz hunt up travel-food," he meow-barked.

Shep glared at Daisy's retreating rump. "You think I'm a good alpha, don't you, Fuzz?" he grunted.

Fuzz didn't even blink. "Shep-dog try. Rarely succeed. But nose on right scent."

Shep stifled a growl, then sighed. *At least the cat's honest.* "I just don't understand the rush to go home," he woofed. "Why don't my friends feel what I feel?"

The cat considered Shep for a heartbeat. "Fuzz stay with Shep-dog," he meowed. He nodded his pink nose and purred loudly.

"An ex-alpha and a declawed cat," Shep groaned. "We'll be quite a pack."

Fuzz stopped purring. "Shep-dog no want Fuzz?" the cat hissed.

Shep wished he'd kept his snout shut. Nothing he woofed was coming out right. He'd just kicked dirt in the snout of his most loyal packmate.

"Of course I want you in my pack, Fuzz," Shep woofed. "You're the only friend I've got."

The cat flicked the tip of his tail, thinking. "Accept apology," he meowed.

Shep wagged his tail. "I'll howl the pack together," he barked. "We'll move straight through the Park toward sunrise. Will you scout ahead, see if there's any trouble lurking?"

"Fuzz check," the cat meow-barked and sprang off into the shadows.

Shep gathered the dogs, gave them each one of Fuzz's bug snacks, and explained the formation he wanted to move in.

"I want Dover and Boji to take the flanks, and Daisy, you take rear point." He turned his snout to Zeus. "You stay in front of Daisy."

"Aye, aye," grumbled Zeus in a lazy drawl, as if this was all boring. As if organizing the pack wasn't the most important step in moving a group of dogs. *Then again, Zeus's wild pack was like a litter of pups — every dog running whichever way their noses took them. And that's why his pack was defeated. Organization is critical —*

"This is a bad idea," yipped Pumpkin. "A super-bad idea."

"What is it, sweet snout?" yapped Ginny. Shep wondered if he should keep those two from woofing. The last thing he needed was for Ginny to help Pumpkin become an even bigger burr in his fur.

"We're going to look super scary to a human, moving as a big pack," Pumpkin continued. "I think we'd do better moving as one or two dogs, you know, just casually loping on the Sidewalk like it's no big deal."

"How am I supposed to defend the whole pack when it's broken into bits and scattered all over the street?" growled Shep.

"Defend us?" yipped Pumpkin, unaffected by — or ignoring — Shep's tone. "From what? The key, I thought, was to make it to the beach without getting nabbed by the dog catchers."

"She does have her teeth in something with that," muttered Ginny.

Shep growled to himself. He was feeling a bit like maybe he should have left the little white fluffy ball of contradictory opinions in her cage.

"We stay in formation through the Park," he snapped. "When we reach the street, I'll reevaluate."

Callie gave him a concerned sneer, one snaggletooth

caught on her jowl. Zeus snickered, betraying his enjoyment at seeing any obstacle in Shep's path.

Shep took his position at the front of the pack, careful to keep Zeus's scent directly behind his tail. *I've got my nose on you, Zeus,* Shep thought. *You'll have to work pretty hard to pull the bedding over this dog's snout.*

Shep kept the dogs under the cover of the trees, moving directly toward sunrise, and soon ran into a wide road. Fuzz caught up with the pack and said that he'd run up and down along the road, and that it was the same one they'd crossed under through the tunnel.

"Road swing away from cold winds, then back toward sunrise," Fuzz hissed. "Dog-pack follow road, yes?"

"Good find, Fuzz," Shep woofed.

Fuzz flicked his tail, then sprang ahead of the pack along the road.

The cat's loyalty to him confounded Shep. Fuzz had every right to hock hairballs at Shep for what he'd done. Shep had tossed the cat and Honey out like ripped toys, abandoned them to be killed by Zeus. Fuzz never meowed anything about it, never asked for an apology, but how could he not blame Shep for Honey's death?

Shep wondered what Fuzz would do once they found the shelter. He said he would stay with Shep, but when he saw his family, would he go home, too?

Shep led the dogs farther under the trees but followed the road's curve away from the cold winds. The woods were fairly quiet — there was an odd lack of life. He took a deep scent of the air and pricked his ears.

"What — *snort* — has got your tail in a twist?" barked Daisy.

He smelled that familiar scent: death and dirt.

Wild dogs.

"Get back in formation," he growled. "And get ready to run."

Shep smelled Zeus become more anxious. He must have scented his old friends. *I'm sure they'll have some questions for you. . . .* Shep thought.

Shep caught the scent closer, near a rotting tree some twenty stretches off.

"To the road," he yipped to Daisy. "Now!"

The pack bolted away from Shep, all except Zeus, who stood with him.

"Did you not hear me?" Shep barked.

"Oh, I heard you," Zeus growled.

There was just one wild dog, but it was bounding toward them. In the moonlight, Shep could tell that the dog was injured. He sniffed and smelled that the dried lifeblood he'd scented before was the dog's own.

"Get out!" snarled the dog.

He was skinny. Too skinny. And he had a ragged collar around his neck. This wasn't a wild dog; this was someone's pet gone wild. The dog was missing a paw — his front leg ended in a jagged wound. He had one, maybe two suns left before the Great Wolf came for him.

"We're just passing through," Shep growled, not angrily, just to let the dog know that he'd defend himself if he had to.

The dog looked from Shep to Zeus and back. His jowls trembled over his bared teeth and his hackles shivered along his exposed spine. Then the dog sprang at Zeus — why, Shep had no idea. The dog had to sense that Zeus could kill him with a single swipe of his fangs, which Zeus did. The dog fell to the ground, limp as a stuffed toy.

"You didn't have to kill him," Shep woofed.

"A dog attacks me, I kill it," Zeus snapped. Then he lowered his head and nosed the ear of the fallen dog. "Anyway, this one wanted to die."

"I guess better to die by a fellow dog than to starve alone," Shep woofed. Then he shook his head. Why was he woofing with Zeus like a friend? Zeus was his enemy. Shep could never forget that. He could never let his guard down again.

"Let's get the others," he barked.

The Park opened into a field packed with lakes. Along the banks of each lake lay countless water lizards. Any one of the beasts could have swallowed Pumpkin or Callie whole. *This explains the wild pet's missing paw.* Shep couldn't defend the pack from that many water lizards. He decided to risk leaving the Park and climbing onto the big road.

A fence divided the road from the Park, but the storm had broken it in several places; the metal mesh sagged on its support poles. It was fully night now — the Silver Moon hung high in the sky, sparkling in the tiny stones embedded in the roadway. The darkness would help to keep them hidden.

"Keep to the edge of the pavement," he woofed.

The pack, scared after running into the wild pet and perhaps reminded of what Shep had done for them over the last moon-cycle in keeping them from such a fate, didn't argue. Even Pumpkin kept her snout shut and stayed in formation along the side of the road.

Shep's mind, however, was full of howls. He reminded himself of how strong and fierce and cunning he was, of how many beasts he'd bested over the last moon-cycle, and yet the image of the wild pet could not be chased from his mind. Surviving alone in the city was not going to be easy — particularly with humans barging back onto the streets. Shep wondered if that wild pet had been driven into the Park. What dog would choose to live with all those monster water lizards? Was that really the life he wanted?

The dogs moved slowly, careful where they placed each paw. The road led into an area of wide, low buildings. The buildings looked flimsy; the fact that they hadn't been flattened by the wave confirmed for Shep just how far they were from the beach. But the storm itself had left its scratches. Pieces of wall were missing from the buildings and some were missing their roofs. Light poles lay like sticks across the smaller roads and thick wire strings dangled between them on the stone.

There were only a few Cars sleeping on the vast stretches of pavement next to the buildings, and the air was empty of any scent of life. No Cars rumbled down the wide street the dogs walked on. It seemed their only company was the Silver Moon and the blinking fires in the Great Wolf's coat.

"I'm hungry," whimpered Oscar.

Shep's stomach growled in response. He sniffed the air — a faint scent of food reached his nose. It came from one of the buildings, down one of the smaller streets.

"There's food over there," he woofed, waving his snout toward the scent. "Let's sniff it out and see if we can steal a bite."

Fuzz bounded ahead of the pack, a black blur against the street. The dogs caught up with him near a window.

"Food here," he hissed. "Boxes and boxes. But window closed, door closed."

Callie stuck her nose to the wall and began scenting for another way in. "I found something!" she yipped from around the corner.

Shep found her pawing at a broken piece of siding.

"I think we can dig through the wall here," she woofed. "It's made of thin metal. If we pull on it with our paws and teeth, I think we can bend it back far enough to sneak through."

Shep dug his teeth into the broken strip and tugged. His teeth slipped for a heartbeat, but then caught on a ragged bit. He jerked his head and the wall peeled back slightly.

"Go!" he grumbled through his teeth. The pack squeezed through the opening.

Inside, the only light came from the small windows and a dim bulb near the door.

Callie was the last through, and she waited for Shep inside the hole. "Dawn is still a ways off, so I think we can rest here for a while," she said. "But we should clear out well before the sun is in the sky." From the light pant under her bark and the flutter of her eyelids, Shep could tell that this was a request — Callie was exhausted.

"Sounds good," Shep woofed, happy to hear her barking with him about a plan as if they were still teammates, whatever the real reason.

The others sniffed around the boxes. Zeus tore into a box and found small boxes inside the big one, then sealed bags inside the small boxes.

He bit into one of the bags and grimaced. "It's food," he grumbled. "But it tastes like a stale biscuit."

*   *   *

The pack ate and snoozed in fits. Shep couldn't sleep — he needed to keep an ear on Zeus and a nose on this building, which was bigger than the kibble den and dark as the Black Dog's hide. He paced between the piles of boxes, row upon row of the stale bags of food. Shep had choked down a whole bag of the stuff. He guessed that it was the human equivalent of dry kibble — they'd only eat this if they had no other options. He panted to himself, *What a snob I've become.* This kibble would have been like food from the Great Wolf's bowl when he was in the fight kennel. After eating fresh meat and scraps for so long he wondered how any of them could ever go back to bowl after bowl of dry pellets, for the rest of their suns.

He checked in with each dog to make sure that they were safely snuggled. As he rounded a corner near where they'd snuck through the wall, he heard Callie mumbling with Fuzz.

"*Snnnnnnurlllllll,*" she growled.

"No," hissed Fuzz, "Callie-dog use too much jowl."

Callie shook her head, then pursed her jowls. "*Snnnuuuuuuuuuurrrrrrl,*" she cooed.

Fuzz purred loudly. "Not terrible." He licked a paw and ran it over his ear, a smile curling across his muzzle.

"What are you two doing?" Shep woofed.

"Fuzz is teaching me to speak cat," Callie yipped, her curved tail waving.

Shep's jaw nearly fell from his head. "What in the name of the Silver Moon has possessed you to learn *cat*?" he barked.

"My family has a cat," she woofed. "I thought it'd be nice, once I was home, to be able to bark with her."

Callie had never mentioned a cat before.

"Some dogs think cat interesting," Fuzz meow-growled.

Shep snuffled the fur near Fuzz's ears. "I think you're interesting," Shep woofed. "But why not teach the cat to speak dog instead?"

"Silly fur, how am I supposed to even ask her if she'd like to learn dog if I can't speak cat?" Callie panted gently. "Anyway, I want to learn a few woofs, so she knows I want to be her friend." Callie licked her front dewclaw. "We didn't start off on the right paw, if you catch my whiff."

"Few dogs do," grumbled Fuzz.

Callie explained how when her family brought her home, the cat was already in the den. Her name was Misty and she was an older cat, one of the meowers who yowled in the alley and drove Shep to gnaw on his toys to keep from chewing his fur off. Callie's puppy brain had thought Misty was a toy, like a stuffed cat that could move. She tore after Misty, chasing her up the walls and the curtains and on top of the cold box. The cat began losing patches of fur out of nerves. She hid behind the woman's legs, clawing her way up the human's pants whenever Callie so much as sniffed at her.

Callie had thought this was the most wonderful game ever invented. Only the Red Dot was more fun, but she needed her girl to play Red Dot. Chase the Cat was a game that could be played whenever the mood struck.

"So you can smell why maybe I need to put in some extra effort if I want to get Misty to like me." Callie looked at both Shep and Fuzz.

Fuzz nodded his muzzle, as if considering the matter on Misty's behalf. He sat in his compact fashion, tail curled neatly around his paws. Its end flicked slightly in time with his purr.

"Well, good luck," Shep woofed.

He lumbered into the dark again but gave up his pacing. He slumped down next to one of the boxes, tore a strip of the box-paper off, and began to gnaw on it.

Callie was learning cat. *CAT!* So that she could go home and make friends with something she considered prey a few moon-cycles ago. Why would she want to go back to that? Fine, she'd have food and a bed and a girl to protect her, but how could that life compare to running free with him? Hunting in the woods? Great Wolf, she wanted to bark with a *CAT!* What next, was she going to ask Pumpkin for tips on how to get her tail to curl better? Where was the girldog who'd tear through a mud puddle to chase down a scrap of paper? Who clawed through a screen to eat a lizard? What happened to *his* Callie?

A faint jangling stirred Shep — he couldn't believe he'd dozed off. He twitched his ears and took a deep scent of the space. The pack was still snuggled in their makeshift beds around him. Something jangled again, louder.

"Shep-dog!" Fuzz dropped from the box above Shep to the floor. "Human at door!"

Shep sprang to his paws. The sky was lightening Outside, and he saw through the small window a man's helmeted head and green-clad shoulders against the pale clouds. Men in green — *dog catchers.*

He had only heartbeats to get his friends out of the building. The whole pack couldn't squeeze through the hole in the wall without at least some dogs getting caught by the men. Shep had to find another means of escape.

The door. But that would involve some dog — most likely him — knocking over whomever was jangling on the other side of it. He knew that no dog would forgive him for that — he wasn't even sure he *could* knock over a human again.

A part of the wall squealed, then started to rumble and roll itself up, creating a sliver of open air between it and the floor. Enough room for the whole pack to bolt out of!

"Dogs!" Shep barked. His voice echoed throughout the space. "Race for the growling wall!"

His pack awoke in a heartbeat and dashed down the aisles. Shep watched them run, then tried to locate the humans. He had to make sure every dog escaped.

A hand grabbed his scruff.

"Dogs!" a man shouted.

Shep yelped and struggled free of the man's thick fingers. He scrambled away, heart racing. The other dogs were already squeezing out from under the growling wall, which screeched to a halt. The wall squealed again and began to drop. Shep ducked his head under the rattling metal and escaped into the cool morning air.

"Keep running!" he howled to his packmates. "They're men in green!"

Every dog's eyes widened — the scent of their terror rose like a cloud. The pack bolted for the roadway. Snoop pulled ahead of the rest, his sleek body curling and stretching in long, springing strides. Shep sniffed to make sure all the dogs were ahead of him and smelled Callie far behind.

"Callie!" he cried, wheeling back toward the building.

Callie stumbled along, running as fast as her still-sick body could manage. Shep snapped his teeth around her scruff and, tugging with every bit of strength in his neck, pulled her up. Sure of his grip on her fur, he sprinted after the others.

"Thanks," Callie wheezed.

"We're not safe yet," Shep growled through locked jaws.

They were almost at the street. The other dogs had already reached the Sidewalk.

Daisy stopped suddenly, her paws skidding on the gravel. *"Car!"* she howled.

But it was too late.

The huge Car roared down the road, as fast as the wave. Snoop barely had time to look up.

"SNOOP!" shrieked Pumpkin.

A dull thud. The Car raced on.

There was no trace of Snoop.

CHAPTER 9
LESSONS RELEARNED

Shep's jaws unlocked and Callie dropped onto the grass. "Stop!" he howled.

As if in response, the Car squealed to a halt. One of its doors opened, and a shrieking human stumbled out. Shep tensed his muscles and scented the air: They were caught between advancing men in green and a screaming person hidden by a giant Car. The scent of spilled lifeblood reached his nose; he stopped sniffing.

"He's a dog catcher!" Rufus yelped.

The human shuffled around the side of the Car, bearing Snoop's limp body in his arms. The men in green ran past Shep and the other dogs to help the man lift Snoop into the Car.

"Are we waiting to see how long it takes them to come for the rest of us?" Zeus snarled.

Shep growled at the boxer, then stood tall, ears up and tail rigid. "Back in formation!" he barked. He would not let them take Callie!

The pack, still shocked and trembling, fell in behind his tail. Shep raced them down one of the small roads and alongside a large building.

"We have to stop!" barked Callie. She flicked her tail at Pumpkin. A newcomer to the horrors of the drowned city, the poor girldog was in terrible shape. She cowered low to the pavement, shivering, and twitched her ears.

"We were just barking together," she mumbled. "He wasn't even really in the street."

The pack huddled around her. Shep knew he should woof something, but his mind went blank. It was his fault that Snoop had run into the road; he'd commanded the pack to rush out of the building without so much as scenting to smell if all was safe Outside. The screaming man hadn't meant to hit Snoop; Shep smelled how sad and scared the man was. The miserable human had just driven by at exactly the wrong heartbeat. It was Shep's failure as an alpha that put Snoop in front of the Car. This loss lay squarely across his withers.

"It's my fault," he woofed. "I shouldn't have barked for you to run without scenting for danger."

"Stop being such a fur-brain," Zeus snapped. "We all know the street's dangerous. The dog should've stopped at the Sidewalk."

"His *name* was *Snoop*!" Shep snarled and lunged at Zeus.

Oscar jumped in front of the boxer. "He's hurt!" the pup cried.

Shep threw his weight to the side to avoid Oscar. "Have you completely lost your tail?" Shep growled, panting.

Oscar stared down his snout at Shep. "Zeus might be mean, but he's hurt. It's not a fair fight." Then he lowered his tail and ears. "We all know it wasn't your fault that Snoop got hit by that Car. That's all Zeus was trying to woof."

Shep lowered his hackles. The pack seemed frozen in their fur. They smelled frightened and anxious — Shep had only made things worse. Even Zeus appeared unnerved by Shep's attack. *An alpha doesn't attack his pack*, he thought to himself between pants. *Even those pack members he hates.*

"You're right, Oscar," Shep woofed, calming himself. "I'm sorry, all of you."

Daisy loped to Oscar's side and gave him a snort. "That took guts, pup," she woofed, smiling. "But you get in the alpha's way again and I'll snap you like a biscuit."

Oscar, who'd begun wagging his tail, stopped.

Callie stepped between them. "We're all just upset about Snoop," she woofed. She trotted up to Pumpkin, who was so shaken she'd practically trembled all the hair from her body. "That man will help Snoop," Callie snuffled. "He'll take him to the kennel and they'll fix him the way they fixed me."

Dover sat on Pumpkin's other side. "Snoop may not have looked it," he woofed, "but he was tough as rawhide. He'll be back to playing Big Stick and Diggin'est Dog in no time."

Ginny panted lightly. "Do you remember during the storm, when he knocked that big bush on my back?" she yipped, her ears up. "Even when he wasn't trying to play, Snoop managed to put a wag in every dog's tail."

Rufus snickered. "I don't remember your tail wagging after being smushed by that plant."

Ginny gave Rufus a playful nip. "With time, I've seen how such a thing could be funny."

Boji sat beside Dover. "Snoop is tough. He helped me to lick wounds," she woofed. "And once, Higgins yelled at him for giving an extra kibble to a hungry new rescue, so Snoop nosed his whole ration to the starving dog."

Fuzz began purring loudly. "Fuzz always like skinny-snout," he meowed. "Less fuzz head than most dog."

All the dogs began to smell more relaxed as they woofed about Snoop. Tails wagged and smiles played across every dog's snout. Pumpkin stopped trembling and stood a little taller.

"Who's this Higgins you keep barking about?" she asked.

"Now there was a dog who knew the kibble from the trash!" howled Rufus.

The pack started walking again, each dog yipping some hilarious tale about their former packmates — friends who were gone, but never forgotten. Shep couldn't help but wag his tail remembering the way Higgins's furface would bristle whenever he got frustrated. He even shared a story of his own, telling how Virgil rescued him in the stairwell from the fury of the storm.

As they loped down the Sidewalk, Shep didn't need to bark for all the dogs to stay together. The pack huddled close, barking and yapping and wagging their tails. All save Zeus, who lagged behind, limping. His muzzle was frozen in a mask of disdain, but Shep swore he saw Zeus's jowl tremble and his eyes blink each time some dog woofed Higgins's or Virgil's name. In that heartbeat, Shep wondered if perhaps Zeus really was sorry for having killed them. In the next heartbeat, he reminded himself that he didn't care if Zeus was sorry. *He'll never be anything but a killer.*

The large buildings gave way to smaller ones, and soon the streets were lined with regular, boxy human dens. They saw a few humans digging trash from their yards and one or two Cars chugged by, loaded down with bags and salvaged pieces of furniture. Shep avoided any humans he smelled by crossing to a new street; every dog flinched when a Car passed.

As the sun crossed its midpoint, the pavement became unbearably hot under their paws. They needed to find water.

Shep had just decided to risk a rest when Boji barked, "I smell fresh water. And grass. Just off the road." She waved her tail, hopeful.

"Fuzz, check it out," Shep woofed, waving his snout.

"I'll go!" yipped Oscar. The pup dove into the scrubby hedge and got caught in a thatch of branches.

As he untangled himself, Zeus grunted a quick pant, then went back to scowling.

The cat hissed, then disappeared over the hedge in a single spring. After a few heartbeats, he meowed through the leaves. "Very strange. Huge Park with pits of sand and lakes. Grass pokey and short like shave fur."

"Humans?"

"No. Safe for dog-pack."

The dogs pushed through the broken and tangled branches of the hedge. Tall metal posts showed where a fence had once stood, but the dogs were able to pad onto the open field without facing any greater obstacle than the bush.

The field was narrow, but the grass stretched away on either side of Shep farther than he could smell. The green had been cleared of garbage; bags were piled neatly at regular intervals between the sparse trees lining the field's edge. From the intensity of the scent, Shep guessed the grass had been clipped within the last sun.

As Fuzz had meowed, the field itself was pocked with irregularly shaped pits and ponds. Several stretches away, on a small hill, a narrow pole stuck up from the ground. The strip of cloth at its top billowed in the breeze.

The strangeness of the open space unnerved Shep — what was this huge Park doing in the middle of all these dens, and why was it so clean and neat when everywhere else was still trashed from the storm? "We get a drink, then meet back at the hedge," Shep barked. "No playing. No barking."

The others smelled just as anxious. They slunk along the tree line, then scrambled to the water. The dogs drank quickly, glancing up after every few slurps to scan the grass.

Shep hung back, watching, until every dog had gotten a drink. He waved his snout at Daisy and had her take over the watch. Just as he wet his nose, she barked for him. He snuck a quick sip of water, then skulked, belly to grass, back to where she stood near the hedge.

"I heard something," Daisy snorted. "A motor. Up toward the cold winds along the grass."

Shep scanned the rolling hills of the field.

"Keep watch," Shep woofed. "Last drink!" he barked to the others.

He loped back to the pond and took a long drink. He wasn't sure when they'd find another source of clean water — he couldn't even be sure what they'd find around the next tree.

He heard a motor, but it sounded small. Then a tiny, boxy white Car with no doors, just a white plastic roof held up by metal branches, burst out of the trees. A young man in dark blue body coverings hung out the side of the Car. He was waving a thin metal stick with a fat paw on its end and yelling, "No dogs!" Then he shouted something else, but all Shep could make out was the word "Go."

Shep didn't know where this man specifically wanted them to go, but he clearly wanted them off his grass.

"Dogs!" Shep barked. "Back through the hedge!"

"We can't!" barked Daisy. "There's another one!" She bolted past Shep and sprang over the pond, racing for cover in the trees lining the other side of the open grass.

Shep looked behind him and saw that their entrance through the hedge was blocked by another of the tiny white Cars, this one carrying a different young man in a blue suit. He waved a long stick topped by a fan of metal fingers spread like a wing. What did these men want to do to them? They didn't seem like dog catchers, but Shep was sure that wagging his tail and acting friendly would not calm them down.

Shep dove over the pond. "Follow me!" he howled. He raced across the grass, kicking up clumps of mud.

"Zeus!"

Oscar's cry carried across the wide lawn. Shep whirled mid-stride; Zeus had caught his bandage on a root and was stuck. One of the boxy Cars was closing in on him — and Oscar was running right into its path.

"Oscar, leave him!" Shep cried.

The pup stopped, ears pricked and eyes wide, like he wasn't sure he'd heard Shep right. "You said we never leave a packmate behind," Oscar barked. "An alpha never leaves a packmate behind!"

Great Wolf, Shep growled to himself, gnashing his teeth as he dashed back toward the fur-brained pup and his evil ex–best friend. *Why can't this pup just listen to me?!*

Zeus stubbornly tugged on the paw, which just wedged the wrapping farther up the stick.

"Stop," Shep snarled. "Let me get it."

Zeus snapped at Shep's snout. "I don't want your help."

"Want it or not," Shep growled, "you've got it." He thrust his snout at Zeus's paw and bit the wrapping, cutting Zeus free.

Shep grabbed Oscar by the scruff. "Let's move our tails!" he barked through clenched jaws and tore through the grass.

Daisy had led the others through the sparse woods, which ended at another hedge. Shep glanced behind him, through the thick ribbon of trees separating the pack from the huge lawn, and saw nothing. It seemed that the men in the blue suits had given up the chase.

Pushing through the hedge's web of branches, they found another broken fence, only this one was made of wooden slats.

Callie poked her head through a hole in the fence. "A den," she snuffled. "Looks empty."

Rufus shoved his snout through the hole next to Callie. "Maybe there's food?" he yipped.

"Let's check it out," Shep woofed. Even if there wasn't any food, they could wait inside the den until sunset. Moving in the sunlight was turning out to be as terrible an idea as he'd imagined.

Shep ducked through the fence first. He found himself in a small yard, much smaller than the one they'd just escaped — ten stretches from fence to den. It was dominated by a gigantic, toppled tree. The den had been crushed on one side when the trunk fell onto its roof.

He stepped to the side and waved his tail to signal the rest of the dogs to come through. "One of the walls is broken," Shep barked. "We can get in there."

The pack loped across the grass and up onto the remains of a wooden deck.

Ginny hopped onto a lounge chair and looked through a glass door inside the den. "Looks nice," she woofed. "There's a lovely couch that looks perfect for snoozing."

Callie sprang onto a board that stuck out of the broken wall of the den. "We can get in here," she yipped. She walked up the board, which jiggled with her every step.

Zeus leapt directly onto the broken wall. Now that his bandage was torn, Shep could see the injured paw. The flesh had been stitched together, but lifeblood oozed out of the ragged wound.

Boji should lick that, he thought, but he knew Boji would never go near Zeus. Anyway, after what he did, Zeus could lick his own stinking wounds.

More than licking, though, the wound needed to be rebandaged. How in the name of the Silver Moon was he supposed to manage that?

The others followed Zeus and Callie into the den. When every dog was inside, Shep clawed his way up the crushed wall and followed them.

The wall opened into the den's food room, which had been thoroughly drenched by the storm. The cold box lay on its side, having been knocked over by the collapsing wall. Other animals had scavenged there; little was left in the lower cabinets or the cold box.

Callie hopped onto the cold box, then up onto the counter. She sniffed the upper cabinets. "There's some food in these," she yipped. She stood on her hind paws, but couldn't get the door to open. "Shep?" she woofed. "Could you lend a paw?"

Shep stood on the cold box and managed to claw open the nearest cabinet. "This is all I can reach," he barked, stretching as far as possible.

"Move out of the way, yapper," Zeus snarled.

Callie hopped back, more out of shock at Zeus's proximity than because he'd said to.

Zeus batted at the cabinet with his good paw and the door swung open. "You're welcome," he grumbled, dropping back onto all fours.

"Thanks," Callie growled, scowling at the boxer.

Inside, Callie sniffed out a box of dry, crunchy twists of dough. There were also some jars, which she knocked to the floor, smashing them in half.

"Let's eat!" she yipped, wagging her tail as she surveyed the meal.

"Dry pasta? Pickles?" whined Pumpkin. "I'm supposed to eat this?" She pawed at a fat green pickle. It rocked back and forth in a puddle of juice.

Ginny flounced off the couch and trotted next to Pumpkin. "It's food, sweet snout," she yipped. "Eat it or step away so I can."

A door creaked somewhere in the den.

Shep glanced around, checking to see who'd strayed from the pack. "Fuzz?" Shep woofed.

"Fuzz here," the cat hissed from on top of the cabinets.

A form took shape in the shadows at the far end of the room. Tall body, thin arms, round head: A human.

"Out!" the person shouted. The woman was old — she had white hair and wore a flowing pink body covering. She held a broom in her bony hands. "Get out!" she cried, her voice cracking.

The dogs panicked. Boji and Dover bolted away from the old lady, scrambling farther into the den. Ginny and Rufus froze where they stood near the food, as if contemplating whether they should stuff their snouts before running. Zeus growled like he was going to fight the woman. Daisy nipped Oscar, chasing him out from under Zeus and onto the crushed wall behind Shep. Callie ran along the counter, sprang over Shep's back, and followed Daisy and Oscar out.

"Fuzz, get Boji and Dover!" Shep barked.

The cat bolted along the tops of the cabinets, then dove into the darkness of the main room.

Pumpkin, the fur-brained fluff ball, pranced toward the old woman, tail waving. "We're just looking for a place to snuggle!" she yipped happily.

The girldog apparently couldn't scent a crazy human from a normal one. This old woman wasn't going to just drop her broom and start sharing treats.

Shep barked his most threatening bark. Even Zeus glanced back at him with surprise. The old woman's eyes widened, exposing their red-veined whites, and she stumbled back. The broom trembled in her hands.

Shep dove forward, grabbed Pumpkin by the scruff, and ran for the broken wall. "Move it!" he growled to Ginny and Rufus as he passed.

Pumpkin wailed as she dangled from Shep's jaws. "How could you?" she cried. "Barking like that at a human. You scared that old woman to death!"

"She was about to beat you into a pile of hair," growled Shep. He ran down the street, hoping the rest of the pack followed.

"She was not!" Pumpkin yapped. "I could have calmed her down. You didn't even give being friendly a chance!"

"Shut your snout before I shut it for you," Shep snarled. He was sick of hearing about how unfriendly he was. He'd just saved the girldog. She could at least pretend to be grateful.

Shep turned up a narrow street in front of a den that led into a covered but empty shed. It smelled strongly of Car, but there was no Car sleeping in the little, open den.

"We rest here," he woofed, dropping Pumpkin on her self-righteous rump.

Callie was the first to arrive behind them. A scowl twisted across her muzzle. "Didn't we woof about you not attacking any more humans?"

"See?" snapped Pumpkin, sitting as straight as possible and cocking her tiny head.

"How would you rather I handled the old woman?" Shep grumbled to Callie. "I just wanted to scare her so she'd back off. I had to grab the fur-brained friendliness patrol."

Zeus lumbered into the den. "Not that any dog cares," he woofed, "but I agree with Shep. Better mean than sorry."

That's just *what I needed*, Shep growled to himself.

"She was old!" yipped Callie. "Would you ever growl at some old timer dog?" She tilted her head in her knowing way, like Shep was an idiot puppy in desperate need of training.

"You want to be the alpha," he barked, "then be one. But until then, I make the calls on how to handle threats to the pack."

Daisy and Oscar appeared next. The pup was whining that Daisy had nipped him too hard, but Shep wasn't about to start messing with Daisy. She was the only dog who seemed to listen to his woofs without barking back about his every decision.

Rufus and Ginny loped in, followed by Fuzz with Boji and Dover.

"Fuzz find second exit through window," the cat hiss-barked. "Save big dogs."

Dover wagged his tail. "That you did, cat."

Fuzz licked his nose. "No need to thank Fuzz," he meowed. "Fuzz just doing helpful duty."

"Not that any dog seems to care," yipped Ginny, flashing Shep a contemptuous look, "but the old woman is fine. Rufus and I made sure Shep hadn't scared the hair from her head."

"Every dog needs to get off my tail about that old woman," Shep growled.

"No," snapped Pumpkin. "You need to rethink your strategy! This is exactly what we were working on back in the Park. You need to think back to before the storm, back when you weren't a menace to society — and here I'm woofing about *human* society.

"I don't care what you've been through during this storm," Pumpkin went on, barking so fast Shep couldn't get a woof in if he tried. "From what you've barked, it sounds pretty terrible. But the city is returning to the way it was *before* the storm. You all need to remember what you were like before all this wildness got into you." She glared into every dog's snout. "We need to start acting like the pets we are and not the wild things you had to become to survive."

Shep was about to finally bark her into submission, but Callie nipped him in the shoulder.

"She's right," she woofed. "You may not like what she's barking, but Pumpkin's right."

Shep looked around at the pack. They all wagged their tails at what Callie said — all except Zeus. That Zeus was his only ally was not a good sign.

Dropping into a sit, Shep licked his jowls. "Fine," he barked. "I'll try a friendlier approach."

Pumpkin snorted. "Don't try," she yapped. "Just *be* friendly. And maybe we won't end up back in the dog catcher's cage."

CHAPTER 10
TO THE BEACH

The dogs snuggled together in small groups around the edges of the Car-den, all except Zeus and Shep, who sat on opposite sides of its open front. Between Shep's paws, several ants were trying to carry a crumb of moldy bread. They moved efficiently; if one ant dropped a corner, the next ant picked up the edge and the food moved toward wherever they were taking it. The ants worked together but seemed indifferent to each other. Shep glanced around at his pack.

Callie was curled next to Fuzz, who barked her next lesson in cat. Fuzz licked Callie's ears as she repeatedly garbled a meow. Boji and Dover played in the corner with a striped stick they'd found in the Car-den. Even an emotional stuffed-nose like Shep could see how much these four cared for one another. After they went home to their families, how would they suffer being apart? And Rufus and Ginny — those two were like jaws: They fit each other perfectly. Didn't they see how great it would be to stay together as a pack? What kept the ants shuffling on, working with bugs they cared less about than a kibble?

Maybe if he'd been a better alpha, his friends would have agreed to stay. Daisy had already woofed so much. Shep smelled her behind him, yapping with Pumpkin about the defense team. Pumpkin couldn't believe that a pug could fight alongside big dogs.

"No offense," the fluffy girldog yipped, "but how could you compare as a fighter with a rottweiler?"

Daisy gave a haughty snort. "It's not about how big you are when you're fighting," she barked. "It's all about your stance, how you present yourself."

Zeus panted from his corner. "Think you could take me, yapper?" he snarled.

Daisy didn't even raise her hackles. "I guess that depends on how long you could survive, missing that front paw." She glared at the boxer for a heartbeat, then continued woofing with Pumpkin.

Shep wagged his tail. He'd turned Daisy from a wimpy pet into a tough-as-claws defense dog. Who cared that he was a terrible show dog and couldn't fake friend-liness to an attacking human — he *was* a good alpha. So why didn't his friends want to stay?

"No one licking your tail tonight?" Zeus grumbled from the opposite corner.

"I don't need any dog to lick my tail," Shep snapped back, curling tighter around his paws.

Zeus panted lightly, then licked his hurt paw. "Every dog likes to have their tail licked," he woofed. "Isn't that why we stick with our humans? So we always have someone to scratch us behind the ears?"

"That's not why I stuck by my boy," Shep grunted.

"You woof 'stuck' like you've moved on from your human," Zeus barked. "So you still think you're going to stay wild?"

"Not wild the way you were wild."

"You think there's another way?" Zeus woofed. "You think you can do anything but be the toughest dog on the street to survive with the wild dogs? Let me clear that scent up for you, friend: You can't."

"I would never become a killer," Shep growled. "I would never hunt down my friends." Then he added, "Former friends."

Zeus grimaced. "True," he barked. "I didn't have to do that."

Shep lifted his head, turning his ears toward Zeus. "Why did you, Zeus?" he woofed. "Why did you attack us?"

Now it was Zeus's turn to shift away from Shep. He rested his head on the other side of his paws; Shep could see nothing but the tips of his ears. "I'm a bad dog," he grumbled. "Bad from claws to jowl."

Something in the way he woofed it made it seem like Zeus wasn't barking all his thoughts on the issue. Shep sniffed and scented that Zeus was anxious and angry and sad, all in the same heartbeat. Part of him wanted to curl next to his old friend, to offer him some comfort, but then he thought of Higgins and Virgil and Honey and all the other dogs who had died at Zeus's command. Zeus didn't deserve comforting.

Shep licked up the ants, dug his nose between his paws, and closed his eyes to the light.

Shep slept in fitful bouts. By the time the sun set, he felt more exhausted than when he had lain down.

"Time to move out," he woofed.

Zeus rose from the shadows. He looked like he'd slept as poorly as Shep. Blaze had once woofed, *The unhappy dog gets no rest from his troubles.* Of all that girldog's crazy beliefs, this was the only one that had proven itself true.

Fuzz appeared at Shep's side. "Fuzz check street," he meow-barked, then skittered down the pavement.

The others woke and stretched, and Daisy began barking them into formation.

"No," yapped Pumpkin. "No formations. We should move in small groups or as single dogs. And I'm not even sure we should all go together. What if we split up and met at the beach?"

Shep smoothed his hackles. The fluffy girldog's every bark set him on edge. "We don't even know how far we are from the beach," he grumbled. "We could wander for suns before we met up again. And what if you ran into a wild dog? Would you be able to charm your way out of a real battle?"

Callie flattened her ears and raised her eyebrows: She was not amused. "I think we can keep within scent of one another without raising any suspicion," she barked. "I haven't smelled, heard, or seen any humans pass the Car-den this sun. It might just be the group of dens we're in, but I think that most of the city is still empty."

Pumpkin gave Shep a hurt look and flicked her tail, as if waiting for an apology. Ginny shuffled to her side and licked her head, offering her some comfort from Shep's bullying. *Great Wolf*, he sighed.

"I'm sorry I snapped at you," Shep grumbled, tail low. He was tired of every dog contradicting his orders. He regained his stance, raising ears and tail, and repeated Callie's idea. "We move in small groups — three dogs at most. Stay within scent-range of me. I will track directly toward sunrise."

Rufus raised his bushy gray ears. "And if we do happen to bump snouts with a wild dog?" he yipped.

"I'll smell it," Shep barked, "and come running."

Oscar, sitting near Zeus's hurt paw, looked at Shep with a smile on his jowls, the old sparkle in his eye. At least some dog still viewed Shep as an alpha.

Fuzz scampered back into the garage. "Street clear," he hissed. "One Car pass. Saw old human in broken den. Broom still in hand."

Shep licked the cat on the head as a sign of thanks. Fuzz cringed, then looked up at Shep like he'd piddled on his fur. The cat licked a paw and began grooming the besmirched hairs.

Pumpkin divided the dogs into groups that would attract the least attention. "We have to balance the cute with the . . . less cute," she woofed, ears pricked and head tilted in thought. "Boji, you go with Zeus and Oscar, and Dover —"

"I will not go with that killer," Boji growled. She began to tremble, as if raising her hackles physically pained her.

Dover licked Boji's nose. "I think I'll stay with Boji," he woofed. "If it's all right with the rest of the pack." He glanced at Pumpkin, ears up and tail flat.

Pumpkin sighed, as if this were a huge problem. "Fine," she snuffled. "Boji, you go with Dover. I'll go with Rufus and Ginny. Daisy —"

"Daisy sticks with Zeus and Oscar," Shep interrupted.

Pumpkin glared at him. "I was just going to bark the same thing. So that leaves you with Callie and the cat." Pumpkin gave him the once-over with her beady black eyes. "I hope they're enough to counter your general growliness."

I'll show you growly, Shep grumbled to himself, but let the girldog's comments go. If Callie thought Pumpkin was on the right scent, then there had to be something to what the fluffy girldog woofed. And the Great Wolf knew, Shep had proven himself worse than Zeus at dealing with the humans they'd encountered so far.

As the last rays of sunlight dulled to deep purple blue, the dogs headed out of the den toward the beach. The moon shimmered in the sky, a fat crescent of white, and already a few fires of the Great Wolf's coat glimmered.

The street wound through a collection of dens, all of a similar size. The dogs traveled undisturbed and Shep couldn't scent any hidden danger, so they stayed together in a loose clump as they loped down the Sidewalk. The storm had barely touched some of the dens; others were missing windows or whole walls. The light of a dim lamp warmed a curtain in one — all the dogs drifted toward its familiar glow until Shep's growl woke them from their trance.

The road swung away from the dens and ended at a larger street.

"We split up here," woofed Shep.

He had Boji and Dover take the lead, followed by Daisy, Oscar, and Zeus. Shep's team left third, with Pumpkin, Ginny, and Rufus at the rear.

"I don't know why we have to go last," grumbled Ginny. "Lassie knows, we can move faster than that boxer."

"Exactly," barked Shep. "I can't have every dog running ahead with Zeus limping at the rear. We need to stay within scent-range of one another."

They moved down the large street in a line and then split off onto side roads. If Shep lost the scent of a dog, he howled their name. After several rounds of howling, the pack had a sense of how far they could wander before they had gone too far.

Callie and Fuzz mumbled woofs in cat back and forth to one another. Shep felt like the odd dog out. He'd hoped that maybe he and Callie could have barked more as they walked, that maybe he could have tried to convince her again to stay with him. But she was oblivious to his entreaties. Every time he barked something to her, she answered in as few woofs as possible. She wasn't unfriendly, just uninterested.

The night passed uneventfully. They crossed under a huge road and heard the *whoosh* of Cars flying down the pavement above them, but the road they followed remained mostly empty. One Car drove by — one of the big, boxy metal machines driven by the men in green — but either it didn't see or didn't care about the three dogs trotting along the pavement. Pumpkin's plan was working: The smaller groups apparently weren't considered a threat by the men in green.

As the sun rose, the road swung toward the cold winds, then ended in a canal. The others had run into the same problem, and they all met up with Shep and Callie at the main road, which had the only bridge as far as any dog could smell.

"I think we should keep going," woofed Pumpkin, who seemed to buzz with energy. "I think I can smell salt. We're getting close to the beach!"

"The canal smells like salt," grunted Zeus.

Pumpkin ignored his downer-dog woofs.

Shep looked around at the others, who waved their tails and looked at him with pricked ears, eager to keep moving. "It's not worth the risk of traveling during sun time," he barked.

Callie placed a paw on his. "We should keep going no matter what the risk," she woofed. "Seeing people back in their dens, I'm worried our humans might leave the shelter. We have to get there as soon as possible."

Shep's tail began to wag. Callie's family might have left the shelter! *My pack might be forced to stay wild!* But the thought that *his* family might not be at the shelter — that he might not even have the option of going home — stopped his tail's swing. It was one scent to woof that he was staying wild, but another track entirely to think he could never go home.

"So we keep going," Shep woofed. He padded out onto the bridge and led his pack onward toward the brightening sky.

*   *   *

Across the canal was an area of larger, flat buildings — stores and storage buildings like the kibble den and the place with the dry-biscuit human food. The streets stretched farther apart to accommodate the sprawling fields of pavement around each building, which made it difficult for Shep to scent the small groups.

Shep glanced at Fuzz. The cat nodded his small head, then burst off to check on the others.

Callie watched him go. "That cat has really come to love you," she woofed.

Shep panted. "*Love* me?" he yipped. "No, Fuzz tolerates me. After what I did to him, to Honey, I feel lucky to get even that."

Callie grinned. "You're not very good at sensing anything other than anger, are you? Always aware of an oncoming attack, but blind to a dog's love." She licked his nose, then padded down the street. "You have to work on that, partner. There's a lot of love that you're missing."

Shep followed her, silent. Was that true? Were there dogs out there loving him and he had no idea? He felt like all any dog did was argue with him. But Callie's woofs reminded him of something Blaze had said to him once, back in the boat. She told him that he needed to believe in himself as much as the pack believed in him.

But the pack had always wanted more from him. He'd always felt like such a failure in their eyes, like he could never be a good enough alpha. Maybe he wasn't able to see love, at least not in other dogs. Growing up in the fight kennel, all there'd been was hate between him and his fellow dog — except with the old timer.

And his boy. His boy had loved him.

Sadness washed over him like a wave. And for some reason, he couldn't push it away. His claws dragged on the stone.

Callie glanced over at him. "What's dragging your tail down?"

"I miss my boy," he woofed. "But I'm not ready to go home — at least, a big part of me isn't. I feel like I'm being torn apart."

"Just keep doing what you're doing," Callie yipped. "Follow where the Great Wolf leads you. Maybe when we reach the shelter, you'll know what to do."

By the time Fuzz caught up with them, the sun was fully in the sky. "Shep-dog!" he screeched. "Trouble!

Evil-dog-of-horrible-deeds has bad paw. Small-snout and smush-muzzle stopped in alley."

Shep and Callie raced after Fuzz through roadways lined with mounds of wreckage from the storm. Daisy barked to them from the mouth of an alley next to a board-covered store.

"It's bad," she snorted. "The fur-brained pup wouldn't let me leave him." She waved her snout toward a large, metal box overflowing with garbage. Shep found Zeus growling with Oscar beside it.

"This will help," Oscar barked. "Just let me put it on your paw!" He held a plastic bag in his jaws.

"It's too small," Zeus growled. He held his paw up against his chest, as if he were guarding it. The remains of the bandage were streaked with red and the wound itself oozed a yellowish goo.

Shep looked at Fuzz. "Tell the others to make for the beach," he woofed. "We'll meet them there." He turned to Daisy and Callie. "You go with Fuzz," he snuffled. "Join Ginny's team and keep them out of trouble."

Daisy's ears pricked up. "Alpha, we can't just leave the pup with that dog."

"Just go," grumbled Oscar. "I'll think of a way to fix Zeus, then we'll follow your scent." The pup kept his eyes on the pavement.

Shep licked Oscar's head. "I'm staying, pup."

Oscar looked up at him, a small grin on his jowls. "Well, only if you want to."

"I'm staying, too," yipped Callie.

Shep's ears pricked. Maybe Callie was beginning to see what he meant about being his partner?

"I could stay," snorted Daisy, "if it would help." She snuck a glance at Oscar.

"You go with Fuzz to tell the others," yipped Shep. "No need for the whole pack to stay on the streets any longer than necessary."

Daisy licked her nose in agreement but did not wag her tail. She looked down at Oscar. After several heartbeats, she snorted, "Stay out of trouble." Then she trotted out of the alley, barking for Fuzz to follow.

"I don't know what you think you can do," Zeus snarled. "The paw's done for. I can't walk."

"Then we'll find another way to move your sorry rump," barked Callie.

Zeus's jowls curled at her yips. "I don't want your help."

"Shut your snout before we start listening to you," Shep woofed. He turned to Callie. "Zeus needs a shoe, what humans wear on their feet."

Callie looked at Zeus's paw, her head tilted in thought. "No," she barked. "I don't think he can walk on that, even with a shoe." She trotted down the alley and began sticking her snout into the various piles of trash. "Oscar!" she bayed. "Get over here and help me sniff for wheels!"

The pup scampered down the alley after Callie's curled tail.

"Why are you helping me?" Zeus growled, squinting at Shep.

"I'm not helping you," Shep snapped. "I'm helping Oscar, and he's got it stuck in his jaw that he's got to help you, so just shut your snout and be grateful."

"Why is that pup hanging on me like some leech I picked up in a sewer?" Zeus dropped to his haunches, then slid across the slimy stone to lie down.

"*That pup* thinks he can make up for betraying his friends by helping you get back to your master," Shep growled. "If not for him, I would have left you to be eaten by a water lizard back in that Park."

"I see you're not interested in forgiveness." Zeus licked his paw and flinched as his tongue hit the wound.

"You don't want to be forgiven," Shep snapped. "You have to be sorry — really sorry — to want forgiveness. You're not sorry, not for anything."

Zeus looked up and for a heartbeat, Shep saw in his eyes something of the old liveliness, the old friend that had run with him through the Park. Shep saw a great sadness, as if that old Zeus was trapped inside this new Zeus, desperate to get out. And then it was gone: Zeus's eyes were again as hard as stone.

"I guess I'm not," he growled. He dropped his head on his paws and stared at the wall.

There was a loud crash and a heap of garbage far down the alley collapsed in a wave of stench. Shep ran toward the pile, sure he was going to have to dig Callie and the pup out. When he got there, he found them tugging on a slimy rope tied to the thick, plastic handle of something caught under the trash.

"Help pull!" Callie barked from between gritted teeth.

Shep snapped his jaws around the rope and tugged back. The trash gave way and out burst a red plastic wagon. The wagon's body had thick, short walls and it rolled on hard, fat black wheels. His boy had had one like it, a dirty old thing that he used to drag his sticks and Balls to the Park to play games with the other boys.

"You want to put Zeus in this?" Shep woofed, dubious.

"You have a better idea?" Callie asked, panting. "My girl had one of these, and she tried to drag me around in it sometimes. It's not comfortable — I always hopped out as soon as I could — but it'll work to move that stubborn, ungrateful, nasty, vile killer you and Oscar insist we help."

"Me? I'm only doing this for Oscar." Shep heard his bark break like a whiny pup's.

"Sure you are," Callie woofed, grinning. "And I'm digging through trash to help Zeus."

They rolled the wagon down the alley toward Zeus, who flicked his horn-ears back like he was going to argue with them. But when Callie barked her idea, Zeus willingly loaded himself into the thing. He had to scrunch into an uncomfortable-looking knot, but somehow the boxer managed to fit into the tiny wagon.

"Let's roll!" yipped Oscar, thrilled at having solved a problem.

Shep looked at Callie.

"You don't think I'm going to pull him, do you?" she yipped.

Shep sighed. "No, I guess not," he barked. He took the mucky rope between his jaws and threw his weight against the wagon. With a groan — from both Shep and the wagon's wheels — the thing rolled forward.

CHAPTER 11
OASIS

Shep rolled Zeus away from the main road, not wanting to attract attention. No human needed to tell him that it was a little unusual to see a dog dragging another dog in a wagon. He kept to the side roads, which were lined with small human dens.

He figured that they were close to the beach, for these dens showed signs of damage from the wave. Swirling brown stains rippled across their fronts and the plants were brown and dying.

"I don't think this was the wave," woofed Callie, sniffing the side of a den. "The walls would have been smashed, like the ones we saw near the boat. This all must have been caused by some other flooding."

"Maybe from the storm itself?" woofed Oscar. "It rained a lot."

"It didn't rain salt," yipped Zeus.

Shep shot him a nasty look. *No need to piddle on the pup's ideas.*

After lugging the wagon for countless blocks, Shep was dying of thirst. "I need a break," he woofed, dropping the rope handle. He glanced up and winced at the hot sun burning over his back.

Callie waved her tail. She scented the air. "Smells like there's fresh water this way."

Leaving the wagon in the gutter, Shep padded toward her.

"What about me?" woofed Zeus, ears pricked. "I need a drink, too."

"You'll have to wait until we find a fresh puddle in the road," snapped Callie.

"I'll bring you back some water!" yipped Oscar. "Don't worry, Zeus." He leapt in the air, trying to give Zeus a lick.

All the dogs looked at the pup like he had grown a second tail. Why Oscar thought meeting Zeus's every need would help the pack forgive him was beyond Shep's comprehension. But the pup really had his teeth in the idea; nothing Shep had woofed so far had gotten him to drop it.

Callie's scent led them behind one of the human dens. Next to the back door sat a large plastic bowl full of water, as if the people had known a couple of thirsty dogs were going to stop by for a slurp.

"Did the humans see us coming?" woofed Shep, suddenly cautious.

Callie sniffed at the bowl. "Smells like it's been here for most of the sun."

Shep scanned the den more carefully. The building itself was intact, but its blue sides bore the brownish streaks that showed where the floodwaters had licked them. The back door of the house had a small hole cut in it at the bottom that was covered with a thick flap of plastic.

"Is that a special hole so animals can get into the house?" Oscar yipped.

"Maybe so one can get out," Callie woofed, head cocked. "Maybe this family had a dog."

Shep glanced around the edge of the lawn but didn't see any sort of fence. "I'm not sure," he woofed.

Oscar trotted right up to the bowl and took a slurp. "Tastes fresh," he woofed. "It must have rained here."

Callie pawed the ground; dust rose around her claws. "I don't think it rained."

The plastic flap in the door moved and a black nose poked out. "Who's there?" a dog woofed.

Oscar startled and tumbled into the bowl of water. "Wild dog!" he yelped, splashing. "Run!"

Shep flicked his tail at Callie, telling her to get behind him. She shuffled a stretch back as Shep took a defensive posture.

The flap lifted completely and out stepped a neat-looking yapper with short, curly brown hair and long ears. "Well, now you've done it, pup," the yapper woofed to Oscar, who flopped in the water bowl. Then he scented Shep and Callie. He looked at them and waved his tail. "Hello!" he woofed. "I'm Murphy the cocker spaniel. You don't smell like you're from around here."

Callie trotted out from behind Shep. "No, we're not," she yipped.

"Callie!" Shep barked. "Get back here!"

Callie kept walking. "He's not a wild dog," she woofed, then asked Murphy, "You're not a wild dog, are you?"

Murphy sat. "Nope," he yipped. "Can't say that I am."

"Then what are you doing here?" Shep growled.

"I live here," he said. "My master and mistress stuck

out the storm in the house. We only left when the water began sloshing in."

"And then did they go to the shelter?" yipped Callie excitedly, her tail wagging. "Can you take us to the shelter?"

Murphy cocked his head at her. "Shelter?" he woofed. "We didn't go to any shelter. We drove to another house that my family often visits, far away from the ocean." The spaniel gave his ear a scratch. "Did *you* go to a shelter?"

Shep sat and stared at his paws. This dog's family hadn't abandoned him; this dog's family took him with them, somewhere far away. Why didn't Shep's family take him with them? Why did the white-shirted man tell them, "No dogs allowed"?

"No," answered Callie. "Our families left us in our dens. We've been surviving on our own for the last moon-cycle."

"It's been two moons," Shep grunted, his bark flat.

Murphy's ears pricked up. "On your own?" he woofed, obviously shocked. "But how?"

Oscar tumbled out of the water dish with a splash. "Through working as a pack and helping each other and fighting for our very lives, that's how," he barked. He puffed out his chest and strutted toward the spaniel.

Murphy's jaw hung open. "Well, I'll be neutered." He looked at each of them, then licked his jowls. "I imagine you dogs are hungry. Let me see if I can get you some kibble." He turned around and popped through the plastic flap-door.

Callie looked at Shep with wide and glittering eyes. "Kibble," she snuffled, slobber drizzling from her jowls.

The door opened and out stepped a woman. Shep hadn't looked at — simply looked at as opposed to evaluated — a human in so long (Did all humans' eyes sparkle? All mouths wrinkle at the corners when they smiled?); for heartbeats, he was mesmerized by her presence.

Murphy barked and leapt at her ankles. She smelled surprised but smiled and said something in a friendly voice. She went back into the den and returned with a huge bag of kibble — just regular kibble, what Shep had eaten every sun for the last cycle, but now, after these moons of starvation and struggle, he swooned at the sight of the bag.

"Hey, dogs!" the woman said in a kind voice. She dropped to her knees and placed the bag beside her. She reached inside the house and brought out a large metal bowl. She placed it on the ground in front of her and then filled it from the kibble bag.

Callie stumbled forward, mesmerized. She looked up at the woman and wagged her tail. "Can I have a bite?" she whimpered.

"Sure," barked Murphy. "It's all for you!"

The woman reached a hand out, gently, cautiously. Callie sniffed it, then gave it a quick lick before shoving her snout into the food.

"Good dog," the woman said, then kept mumbling in a soft voice. She stroked Callie's head and ruffled her ears.

Oscar, unable to resist, dove not at the kibble, but at the woman's knee. "Pet me!" he cried. "Pet me!" He rolled on the ground and leapt again onto her leg.

The woman laughed, then picked up Oscar. The pup wriggled, tail ecstatic, and kissed the woman's cheek. She snuggled him against her chest, murmuring sweetly to him. Oscar looked happier than Shep had ever seen him.

Shep felt frozen in his sit. What if he scared this woman by accident? He tried to remember what Pumpkin had said about being friendly. *Something about lying down? Wagging my tail?*

The woman placed Oscar on the ground, then turned to Shep. She said something in her soft voice and waved her hands, inviting him to come closer.

Shep licked his jowls and ducked his head. He stood and took a small step forward.

"I'm friendly," he woofed as gently as possible.

The woman seemed to understand. She held her hand out for him to sniff, which he did. He waved his tail tentatively, then gave her fingers a quick lick.

"Good boy," she said.

Shep's heart broke at the words. He padded forward, tail waving, and licked her face over and over. The woman wrapped her arms around him. She scratched his scruff and behind his ears. Shep felt a warmth run through him, like his lifeblood had turned to liquid moonstuff. He licked the woman's face, savoring the taste of her skin, human skin. He hadn't realized how much he'd missed it.

He must have come on too strong, because the woman fell back and needed one of her arms to support herself. She pushed Shep off her, but gently, and she was still smiling. He stepped away, hoping he hadn't hurt her.

She pointed to the bowl of food. "Eat," she said. She tousled his ears. He hadn't scared her off.

The three dogs ate until they couldn't choke down another mouthful. The woman watched them for a while, every few heartbeats stroking one of them on the head, then went back inside. Shep heard her voice; it was so nice to hear a regular human voice. After they'd filled their bellies, they drank as much water as they could fit between the kibbles.

"We should go back," Callie woofed, though her voice betrayed that she'd like to stay in this yard forever.

"How will we get some of this back to Zeus?" Oscar yipped.

"Oh, don't go," woofed Murphy. "I haven't played with another dog in so long." He ran to one end of the yard and pulled a well-chewed rope toy from under a bush. "Any of you up for a tug?" he woofed from between clenched jowls.

Shep had to admit that he was tempted, but they couldn't leave Zeus alone in a cart for the whole sun — at least, Oscar wouldn't let them. "Sorry, Murphy," he barked. "We left a dog behind." Shep scooped some kibbles into his mouth and held them there with his tongue. "Thanks," he grunted through locked jaws.

Callie gave Murphy a lick on the snout. "Thank you so much," she yipped. "Please, thank your human for us, too." Her tail wagged with that old enthusiasm.

Oscar slurped water into his snout, then began loping back toward where they'd left Zeus.

A man stepped out from the side of the house into the yard. He was dressed in normal body coverings, but he held a long stick in his hands — a stick with a loop of rope at its end.

A dog catcher.

The woman had been too good to be true — she'd called the dog catchers on them. Shep couldn't let the dog catcher take Callie back, not when they were so close to getting to the beach.

But the man didn't step toward Callie — he was heading directly for Shep. *So the woman did think I'm a dangerous dog.* Shep had pushed his affection too far. This betrayal — the woman's? his own? — hurt him someplace deep inside.

A part of Shep gave up — he could not move. He braced for the man's attack, then smelled Callie's fear. But she didn't fear being caught; she was afraid that Shep would hurt the man. She was afraid *for the human.* Was this what she thought of him? That he was a fighter and nothing more?

Shep gathered his strength. Whatever Callie's opinion of him was, he had to make sure she remained free to return to her family. He'd made her a promise.

"Head for the wagon!" Shep barked. "I'll meet you there!" He burst across the lawn, away from where they'd come, away from Zeus. He'd give Callie and Oscar a shot at escape and hope he could outrun the man.

Spitting the kibbles from his mouth, Shep sucked in a deep breath. He heard the man behind him and slowed his pace so the human could keep up. Shep couldn't let him quit the chase and go back for Callie and the pup.

Shep ran alongside a fence through muddy dirt and dead flowers, then rushed out onto a street. Panting on the pavement, he waited for the human to appear from behind the wooden planks of the fence, then tore down the roadway. Shep saw a hedge three stretches ahead and just as he reached it, he wheeled on his paws and ducked behind its cover. He put all his strength into his legs, pounding across the grass. The human's scent was far behind him and Shep prayed — to the Great Wolf, to whomever — that the man hadn't doubled back on him.

Shep avoided the woman's den — he would not go back there, not even to escape the dog catcher. He dashed across two lawns, hugging the sides of the dens as he passed, then bolted over the street. He rested in the shade of a dense bush on the corner. There was no sign of the dog catcher.

A metal-link fence blocked his path, but Shep found a space where the ground curved away from the wire. He shoved his way underneath it, scraping his skin on a snag in the metal. He pushed through some overgrown weeds and found himself on the street where they'd left Zeus. A few stretches away, Callie and Oscar were tugging on the rope, trying to drag the boxer to better cover behind a Car.

"You need some help?" he woofed, trotting to their sides.

"Shep!" Oscar yowled, tail wagging.

"Quiet!" Callie grunted. "You want to alert every dog catcher in the neighborhood?"

Oscar cowered, then resumed his happy dance in front of Shep, thanking the Great Wolf and waggling his tail.

Callie smiled at the pup, then at Shep. "Knew you'd be back," she yipped quietly.

Shep licked her muzzle. "I promised to get you home, and an alpha doesn't break his promise."

She sniffed, and then her ears twitched. "You're bleeding."

"It's nothing," he woofed. "A scratch from the fence."

"I guess it'd be too much to ask that the alpha brought me back some kibble?" Zeus snorted from his perch in the wagon.

"You guessed right," Shep woofed. Then he took up the wagon handle between his jaws. "Let's get to that beach."

CHAPTER 12
RIP TIDE

Shep pulled the wagon at a trot, though his muscles burned with the effort. He wanted to get as far as possible from that woman and the dog catcher. But also from whatever it was he'd done to scare the woman so. He kept chewing the heartbeats over in his mind, but came up empty-jowled. Why did she call the dog catcher? What had he done?

What's wrong with me?

The road ended at a raised gravel track, on top of which were wooden slats connected by two thick metal humps. Zeus had to get out of the wagon so Shep could bump and drag it over the humps.

Zeus winced as he lugged himself out of the plastic

bowl of the wagon. "This paw is only getting worse," he groaned.

"You want me to gnaw it off?" growled Callie.

Zeus growled back at her. "I'll manage," he grunted.

On the other side of the gravel mound were more streets smelling of salt and rot. The pavement was fringed with heaps of planks, plastic bins, dead plants, and sheets of metal that creaked and wailed in the breeze. The dens beyond were marked with brown swirls up to their rooflines. Rusted tables and chunks of broken stone were strewn among the wilted plants and dead bushes. In some places, the parade of buildings was interrupted by a pile of splintered boards and glass — a den crushed by the storm. As the sun died behind them, no lights flickered on inside these houses.

Callie stopped in front of Shep. "You need to rest," she woofed.

Shep dropped the handle. "We need to meet up with the others."

"Look at your drool." She flicked her snout at his nose. "You're bleeding. You need a rest."

Shep lapped up his slobber. "Fine," he woofed. "But only a short one."

Shep curled next to the wagon — he would sleep, but

only if he knew that Zeus couldn't move without waking him. Shep dreamt he saw his boy. He ran toward him, but was held back. Shep strained toward his boy but couldn't move a stretch. He looked back to see what held him, and there was nothing.

When he woke, it was fully night. Callie and Oscar were arranging a small pile of kibble — mostly garbage, but a small rat topped the mound.

One whiff of the stuff curled Shep's jowls. After all his hunting, all that lifebloodlust, he had one meal of kibble and was transformed back into a pet. He panted, thinking how Blaze would chew his rawhide over being such a dainty-paw.

"You going to eat that or are you having too much fun torturing me?" grumbled Zeus, whose slaver dripped onto Shep's nose.

"Eat up," Shep woofed, shifting away from the fountain of drool.

As Oscar and Zeus dug into the pile, Callie dragged a sealed bag with something rattling around inside it toward Shep.

"It's some sort of human food involving cheese and corn, as far as I can smell." She nosed the bag in front of him. "You need to eat something."

Shep smiled, then rested a paw on a corner of the bag and tore it open with a fang. "Care to join me?"

Callie grinned and lay down at his side. "Don't mind if I do," she yipped.

Shep crunched a mouthful of the cheesy snacks. His boy had liked them — he'd always sneak Shep a few morsels when he ate them. And of course, the heartbeat he thought of his boy, he thought of going home, and thinking of home made him think of that woman and how she'd mistaken his love for aggression.

"Callie?" he woofed.

She looked at him, eyebrows raised.

"Why did that woman call the dog catcher on me?" Shep licked his paw. "I mean, the man was coming for *me*, not you or the pup. What did I do?"

Callie licked her jowls, then snuggled closer to Shep. "I don't think you did anything," she woofed. "The woman cried when you ran. I saw her. I think she thought she was helping us by calling the dog catcher."

Shep lapped up another of the crunchy, cheesy curls. "I keep wondering if I'd been friendlier, whether the white-shirted man would have let me go with my boy."

Callie waved her tail. "If they wouldn't let tiny, harmless Pumpkin stay in the shelter, I doubt the man's decision had anything to do with how friendly you looked."

"But still," Shep grunted. "Even you think I'm monster enough to attack any human that threatens me." He pushed the bag away with his nose. "I saw how scared you were for the dog catcher."

Callie's ears and tail dropped. "I don't think you're a monster, Shep," she snuffled. "I think you'd do anything to protect your pack. When all that threatened us were wild dogs and rats, that instinct of yours saved us. But now . . ." Her bark trailed off. She didn't need to woof that a human — any human, even a man in black — was different.

Callie licked his muzzle and went on, "You're a good dog, Shep. You didn't scare that woman. And you did good by not attacking that dog catcher." Callie cocked her head. "Who knows, maybe by the time we reach the shelter, Pumpkin will have you sitting and giving paw for treats."

Shep smiled. "Let's not get too fur-brained," he yipped.

They loped on through the darkness of the drowned city. In some places, the garbage had been hauled into piles. The roads were lined with mounds of moldy wall scraps, splintered boards, and broken glass and plastic. The humans were trying to reclaim the place from the wreckage. Soon, the street ended in a huge expanse of water.

"Is it the ocean?" yipped Oscar. Shep had forgotten — the pup was so young he'd never even been to the dog beach.

"No," woofed Callie. "You wouldn't be able to see anything across the ocean, and I can see buildings."

"And there'd be a beach," grunted Zeus.

"So we find a way to cross it," barked Shep, taking up the wagon's rope handle.

Shep dragged the wagon to the edge of the water and scanned up and down its shores. It was dark, but the moon shone on the water's surface and revealed two bridges — one not far from where they stood, toward the cold winds.

"We head for that bridge," he woofed.

The bridge itself was long and skinny. Shep barked that they should walk in single file along the edge of the road to keep from being hit by a Car. Callie trembled the whole way, mumbling about how exposed they were and how ridiculous the wagon idea had been.

"This wagon's saved my tail," Zeus grumbled. "I'd say 'thank you,' if I thought you'd hear it."

"Try me," snapped Callie.

"Thank you," woofed Zeus.

Shep heard something in those woofs — a softness? — that made him pause.

"Why are we stopping?" yipped Oscar, whose eyes kept scanning the empty road, sure the dog catchers were only stretches away in the shadows.

"Nothing," Shep woofed and dragged on.

The bridge took them across to a narrow island crammed with buildings, and then to another, and then another, the dens on each going from bad to worse to demolished. As the sky began to lighten, Shep wondered if they'd ever reach the ocean. And then the road shrunk to a path, which dead-ended in white sand. An endless, rippling coat of blue sparkled beyond — "The ocean," sputtered Oscar. They'd made it to the beach.

The horizon at the edge of the ocean was faint yellow and pink, the clouds warming first, then the sky itself. Shep glanced around him — he hadn't been this close to the ocean since before the storm. The buildings told the story of what had happened to them. Shep recalled the beach being lined with tall buildings full of human dens, all sparkling with glass. What remained were jagged teeth of stone, like a broken jaw laid alongside the sand. Some were still recognizable as buildings — a balcony here and there, a window that had somehow held in place — but most were the broken bones that remained after the storm and the wave had torn through. There would be no humans hiding out here to help them.

Shep howled for his packmates, hoping they were within earshot. He didn't want to start wandering around in the sand to find them if he didn't have to, though between the whooshing of the wind and the crashing of the waves, there was little chance any dog heard his call. He hoped they smelled him on the breeze.

Callie was the first to spot some movement down the beach, and then Shep saw them — Boji and Dover, and Daisy and Pumpkin with Ginny and Rufus, and finally Fuzz, slinking along atop the rubble at the edge of the sand. Shep felt joy rush through his fur at seeing his friends. His tail wagged frantically. He couldn't stop himself from giving Fuzz a lick; the cat must have missed him, too, because he purred and waited a whole heartbeat before grooming the slobber away.

Daisy trotted straight to Oscar, flap-ears up and tail waving. The pup cowered and Daisy stopped short. Her tail dropped; she licked her jowls and turned to Shep.

"Alpha," she began. "Nothing to report. We remained hidden under the rubble —"

"We thought you'd never get here!" yapped Pumpkin, interrupting. She wriggled and pranced on the white sands. "We've been here for a full sun, and let me tell you, the beach is not the same as it was!

"First, there are no people. And no food. The beach is also much smaller, like the ocean sucked the sand back into it. And there are weird breaks in the sand now, with rivers of salt water flowing through." Pumpkin seemed completely overwhelmed by the havoc wreaked by the storm. But, then again, she'd spent these last two moons in the kennel — she'd never seen the wave's destruction before.

Daisy glared at the fluffy girldog, one snaggletooth caught on her jowl.

Dover stepped between the two — the look on his muzzle told Shep he'd been doing a lot of crisis intervention between them over the last sun. "Storm damage," he barked. "Just more of what we've already seen."

"What took you so long, anyway?" grumbled Rufus. "And it better have been something terrible because there's nothing to eat on this stinking beach but dried seaweed and I'm starving."

Callie waved her muzzle at Zeus, who was still perched in the wagon. "I guess it depends on what you call terrible," she yipped. "It's not easy to drag a dog across a city."

"What happened to him?" woofed Ginny, snout in the air. "Too proud to walk like the rest of us?"

"My paw's hurt," Zeus growled.

Boji raised her hackles. "We should have left that murderer to be eaten by the water lizards," she snarled softly. Shep thought it was a trick of the wind, that he hadn't heard right, but his nose confirmed it — Boji smelled as angry as the storm.

Callie must not have heard Boji's woofs because she trotted up to where Boji stood, behind Dover. "Would you take a sniff of Zeus's paw? It looks bad."

"I'm not going to lick that monster's wounds." Boji bared her fangs. "I'd tear the paw off before I'd clean it."

Callie stepped back, shocked at the angry scent coming off Boji in waves. "Just tell me if there's anything I can do," she yipped. "You don't have to lick it if you don't want to."

Boji looked to Dover, who licked his jowls and gave a weak flick of his tail. Boji shivered, then padded slowly toward the wagon. She glanced at the paw. "It's not good when it's yellow and stinks like that," she woofed.

"Thanks for stating the obvious," Zeus grumbled.

Boji growled.

"Shut your foul snout, Zeus," Callie snapped. "She's the only one here with real experience healing dogs."

Zeus tucked his paw back into the wagon. "Like licking a wound saved any dog."

"Like I would have had to lick any dog if you hadn't torn them apart!" Boji snarled. She looked at Shep. "What are we doing trying to save this," she gave Zeus a withering glance, *"thing?"*

Oscar puffed out his chest. "Shep promised to help Zeus and me get home, same as you all," he barked. "And it wasn't all Zeus's fault that we're late. We lost half a sun when we met a nice dog named Murphy who was already back in his den with his mistress and she gave us kibble but then she called the dog catcher and Shep nearly got caught!"

"Dog catcher?" snorted Daisy.

"Kibble?" whimpered Rufus, drool dripping from his jowls.

"Already back in their den!" shrieked Pumpkin. "Oh, no! What if my mistress left the shelter? What if she's looking for me *right now*? MISTRESS! I'M HERE! I'M

HERE! *I'M HERE!*" Pumpkin began racing in circles all over the beach, howling and wailing.

"Murphy's mistress never left the shelter," Shep barked, trying to catch Pumpkin as she bolted by. "They were never *in* the shelter." He had to woof something to calm the crazy fluffball down.

Boji's ears pricked. *"They?"* she yipped. "You mean, Murphy stayed with his mistress?"

Oscar scratched his ear. "Murphy's family took him with them to someplace safe to wait out the storm."

The pack seemed to have been smacked by the same giant newspaper — all tails dropped at once. A wave crashed. Foamy water soaked the paws closest to the ocean.

Callie broke the silence. "For the love of treats, we've met one dog — and only one dog — in this whole city whose family found a way to take him with them. Don't let this drag your tails down!"

"Of course we haven't met any other dogs who went with their families!" Boji snapped. "Those dogs didn't need to be rescued. They wouldn't be with the dog catchers. Those dogs' families loved them."

"Our families love us," Callie barked. But the others had already begun to whimper to themselves.

"Our families *chose* to leave us?" muttered Ginny. "I

didn't believe it before, but what if Shep's been right all along?"

"I did piddle on the carpet a couple of times," Rufus yipped, cowering. "My family always got upset when I piddled."

Even Dover sank to the sand. "I *am* getting on in years," he woofed. "Maybe I'm too old to hunt with?"

"Don't even woof such things!" Callie squealed. "You know that your family would have taken you with them if they could have!"

"You *know* that?" Boji snarled. "I don't know that. I know that my mistress and master took their children with them, but they left me behind to die in the storm."

Callie's ears were flat against her head and her tail was between her legs. She licked her jowls nervously. Seeing Boji fall apart shook even Callie's confidence.

Shep padded to Boji's side. The girldog smelled like she was ready to tear her fur from her back. "Your family didn't leave you to die in the storm," he woofed softly. "They thought you'd be safe in the den."

Boji roared on like a thundercloud. "Don't lie to us," she growled. "If it was so safe, why didn't *they* stay? You know as well as I that my family wanted to be rid of me. Who wants a dog who's afraid of steps and doorways?"

Shep dug for something to say. "Well, they should look at you now — you're not afraid of anything! You're ready to go fang to claw with Zeus! You're brave and powerful. If I were your family, I'd be proud to have you back."

Then he looked at all of his packmates and waved his tail. "You're all tough dogs. Maybe that's why our families left us — they knew we could survive. And we have survived!"

Boji panted. "Exactly," she snapped. "They could see the mean parts of us. The parts that could hunt and kill, the parts that could fight another dog. You, Shep, have even fought humans! Our families left us because they saw that we were not really pets. We're wild dogs at the core. Monsters like him." She glared at the boxer with a hate that caused even Zeus to cringe.

Boji's woofs scratched Shep as if she'd actually clawed him. But he knew, somewhere deep under his fur, that she was wrong. Somehow now, he knew.

"I was wrong in the Park when I woofed that we shouldn't go back to our families because they left us," Shep woofed. "I was upset that you all wanted to go home; I said things I shouldn't have."

"What's changed?" yipped Oscar, looking up at Shep with wide eyes.

And upon being asked, he knew. "Meeting Murphy's owner," Shep said. "When she put her hands on my fur, I felt what Ginny woofed about in her story, that connection. We're meant to be with our families."

"You can't know that," Boji grunted.

"I can't know it," Shep barked, "but I believe it."

Callie wagged her tail. "I believe it."

Boji slumped into a sit. "I'm so angry inside, even if they did love me, I'm not that same dog. I've licked hundreds of wounds, seen injured dogs no licking could help. Virgil died at my paws." Boji loosened her stance; the miserable girldog smelled wretched. "I'm broken inside. No family would want what I've become."

Shep licked her nose. "You've become something better," he yipped. "You're a survivor." The idea seemed to brighten every dog's muzzle.

Shep continued, "And your families, they're survivors, too. We've all lived through something terrible. Our families need dogs who can understand what they've been through. They need *us*."

Tails began to wag. The dogs began to snuffle to one another under their breaths.

"Remember when I dropped that brush right on the head of a wild dog?" Ginny yipped.

"I've dug up food from wrecks that would turn the nose of the other schnauzers at the old Park," muttered Rufus, a smile on his jowls.

Pumpkin stared at them all from a perch on a block of stone. "I could totally make a story from this," she woofed, mesmerized.

Dover sat beside Boji, who stared listlessly out at the rolling waves. "Cycles ago, before there was gray in my muzzle, I had a mate, Edie. She could eye a bird better than any retriever I've known. Lost her during a hunt to a water lizard," he yipped. "I was so angry after she was gone."

Boji glanced up at him, gave a small flick of her tail. "What did you do?"

Dover licked her nose. "I used it," he woofed. "Became the best retriever I could be. Never missed a bird, not even if it landed on a water lizard's back."

Oscar began attacking the waves as they rolled onto the shore. "I'm a survivor!" he yelped, diving nose-first into the surf.

"Last one in is a soggy kibble!" howled Callie, leaping into an oncoming wave.

All the dogs began to run in the shallows. Pumpkin pounced on the low waves as they curled up toward the sand and Daisy barked at the swimming silver creatures that floated in the clear tide. Even Zeus hobbled into the surf for a few heartbeats. Spray flew up from the dogs' soaked fur, creating fragile rainbows in the morning light.

Callie jumped on Shep's back, and the two rolled in the wet sand.

"You did it again," she woofed.

"Well, I am the alpha," he barked, tail wagging.

"No," she said. "You're more than an alpha. You're a friend." She nipped his scruff and hopped out into the shallows. "Great Wolf, I'll miss this!" she cried as she bounded through the bubbling surf.

Shep panted. Her woofs broke his heart all over again. They would never again be as free as they were at this heartbeat, and yet he knew now that he would go home, leave this life behind and pick up the pieces of his life with his boy. Somehow, knowing this made him feel both better and worse.

"First dog to nip my scruff gets a bite of the biggest swimmy-thing I catch!" Shep raced up the beach, then wheeled into the oncoming waves. He smelled Boji right on his tail.

"I've got you!" she howled.

Shep pushed off a lump of rough stone on the sandy bottom and felt nothing beneath his paws. The cuts in his fur from the fence stung, but he swam on, digging his legs through the water, swimming deeper, enjoying the strangeness of floating.

"A shepherd can't outswim a retriever!" Boji barked from a stretch or two behind.

There was a tail-wagging tone to her woof; she'd reclaimed some of the happy Beaujolais of yester-sun. Shep looked up at the bright blue of the sky and hoped that he'd made YipYowl and Frizzle and even the Great Wolf himself proud.

Shep turned back toward the shore, sensing his muscles were tiring. Then he felt something huge bump against his chest. A heartbeat later, before he could even process its touch, its teeth snapped around his ribs. He couldn't breathe; the creature seemed to be sucking at his flesh. He dug his paws into the water and his claws hit the thick hide of the monster.

"Help!" he howled.

His packmates' ears all pricked and he saw them all come splashing toward him. His front paw hit sand. Shep dragged himself another step and stumbled. He felt the lifeblood oozing from him; ribbons of red clouded the water. The creature thrashed against his legs, its sharp thorn of a fin slashing the ruddy water's surface. The monster was pulling him down. He couldn't stay afloat much longer.

"Use it!" barked Boji, slamming her paws into whatever held Shep.

And the jaws released him.

Shep saw a gray blur move under the water.

He fell limply into the glassy pool.

Great Wolf . . .

CHAPTER 13
PIECING THINGS BACK
TOGETHER

It was dark. Shep wondered whether he was dead. Above him spun the fires of the Great Wolf's coat. Was he a part of that sparkling blackness?

No, he hurt too much. Thin cuts stung the skin along his belly and sides, and it felt like several of his ribs were broken. Every breath was a pain like he'd just left the fight cage.

"He's awake!" It was Oscar's tremulous yip.

"Oh, thank Lassie and the Great Wolf and every other dog in the sky!" barked Ginny.

The Silver Moon floated bright and full atop the Great Wolf's glittering fur; Shep's packmates shone silver against the night in its glow.

Boji licked Shep's jowls. "You came back to us," she woofed.

Shep lifted his head. "What happened?"

"Some huge fish with a pointy fin on its back!" barked Pumpkin. "We only saw it after it bit you, but holy treats, it was a monster!" She seemed excited, as if he hadn't nearly been turned into kibble.

The pack had dragged him up the beach into the lee of a toppled palm trunk. Callie and Fuzz huddled together under the canopy of dried fronds in front of him. Callie's face sagged. Fuzz was wrapped around himself in a knot of fur.

"We thought we lost you," Callie snuffled. "What would I have done if I lost you?"

Shep tried to lift himself to his paws, but fell back onto the sand — the pain was too great.

"Don't move, you fuzz head," she yipped, shuffling to sit beside his muzzle. She licked his jowls, then his eyes, then his whole snout. "Don't you leave me again."

"I didn't mean to," Shep woofed.

Boji licked his chest. Shep felt her tongue rasp over a cut and winced.

"Sorry!" she yipped. "Just cleaning away some sand."

Shep lifted his head again. "Boji," he grunted. "You saved me."

She smiled and waved her tail. "I used my anger," she snuffled.

"You're a hero," Shep woofed.

Boji ducked her snout. "No," she mumbled.

Dover licked her head like a proud sire. "Don't be modest," he said, nudging her snout up. "You are a hero, Beaujolais."

Daisy snorted a chant, "Bo-ji, Bo-ji," and soon all the dogs were baying her name and running around her in the sand, waving their tails — all except Zeus, who skulked into the shadows. Shep even coughed out a few "Bo-ji's" before his chest hurt too much to move.

After all the stress and worry of the sun, the dogs soon tired. One by one, they came panting back toward the palm trunk. They snuggled near Shep, careful not to touch him.

Shep hid his pain from them as much as he could: He didn't want them to worry. But he wondered whether he was going to be able to make it down the beach anytime soon.

Pumpkin flopped next to his nose. "You know," she woofed, "I misjudged you."

Shep shifted his shoulder to relieve pressure on his ribs. "Really?" he moaned. "You think I'm all friendly now?"

"Not about that, silly fur!" she yipped, then she lowered her head. "I mean, Callie woofed that you've really been working on not attacking people, which is totally snugglelicious." She licked her jowls. "Anyway, I mean I misjudged you as a leader. I really thought you were kind of, well, terrible, what with all the human-attacking and making the others feel bad about going home —"

"Your point?" Shep grumbled.

"You made your pack feel stronger," she said. "What you woofed made a bunch of scared, sad dogs feel brave and loved." She flicked her tail. "Anyhoo, the real point is, you gave me an idea for a story. I finally came up with one of my own! Do you want to hear it?"

"I want to hear it," snuffled Callie from her nest in the sand. The others lifted their heads, ears pricked, to listen.

Once, in the Park, a bright yellow dandelion bloomed amidst the green grass. The sun shone down on the flower, and the flower grew. It burst into a puff of white-tufted seedlings. As the warm breezes blew by the puff, each seed was carried off. The seeds swirled, happy in the gentle winds, and looked down on the glittering world beneath them.

One evening, a storm growled and grumbled. Fierce winds snatched the seedlings away from the gentle breezes. The seeds clung to their white tufts, wondering how they would survive this blustery storm.

The winds swirled into a great spire, and one seedling caught sight of her brother.

"Hold me close!" the seedling cried, and the two seedlings clung together.

More seedlings were sucked into the circling wind, and they all held on to each other for safety. Soon, the snuggled seedlings were again a white puff. It no longer mattered where the winds pushed them — the soft sphere of their tufts protected all the seedlings. They held one another, and in that holding, every seedling kept safe.

The storm died down and the gentle breezes returned. They cried out for the seedlings they loved. Though the seedlings were warm and safe inside the puff, they missed blowing about with their gentle winds. The seeds gave each other one final hug, and then burst apart like an exploding star. Each drifted into its own breeze, and each breeze lovingly caressed its seedling.

When Pumpkin finished, she waved her tail, ears pricked. "What do you think?" she yipped.

Shep looked down at Fuzz and Callie on either side of him, at his packmates around him, and felt warm and loved and sad all at the same time.

"That was a good story, Pumpkin," he woofed.

Pumpkin smiled, then snuggled down into her fur and closed her eyes.

Shep couldn't sleep — everything hurt too much — and he could tell Fuzz was awake, too, keeping watch over him.

"I'm okay, Fuzz," Shep woofed. "You can sleep."

Fuzz flicked his cat-eyes at Shep, then closed them again. The tip of his tail tapped against the sand. "Fuzz have to watch Shep-dog," the cat mewed. "Make sure air go in, then come out."

"Don't worry a whisker about me," Shep snuffled. "I've survived worse." He turned his hips and pain shot up his spine. "Anyway, we're almost to the shelter. You'll have a hard time watching me when you're home with your family."

"Fuzz only family was Honey-friend." His meow-bark broke off as if his lungs had failed him. "Honey-friend was Fuzz home."

"How can a dog be a home?" Shep woofed, not sure why this subject made his skin feel all tingly.

The cat hissed a pant, smiling. "Shep-dog think home is dog-bed? Home is walls and roof and bowl of kibble? No," Fuzz meowed. "Walls of home is walls of heart."

Shep closed his eyes and saw Callie, her muzzle on his shoulder as they stared out the window hole at the storm. He felt Blaze's soft fur against his back. His boy's hand in his scruff. And Fuzz's green eyes glowing in the dim moonlight. This was love. These dogs and boy and cat were his home.

"I understand," he snuffled.

Then he straightened his head so he could look Fuzz directly in the eyes. "I want you to know, Fuzz, you can stay with me."

The cat didn't move; the tip of his tail flicked.

"Whatever it takes to convince my family, I'll do it." He licked the cat's nose. "You're part of my home now," Shep added.

Fuzz ran a paw over his snout, then purred. "Shep-dog part of Fuzz home now, too."

*   *   *

The sun rose in a clear sky — it would be hot later, so Shep barked every dog awake. He wanted to get as much sand under their paws as possible before the sun got over their backs. Now that he'd made up his mind to go home, he was eager to get there.

Shep rolled to get his front paws under him and cried out in pain. Callie and Fuzz were beside him in a heartbeat.

"Shep-dog bleeding," the cat hissed. "Dog-pack must wait!"

"If we wait until I stop bleeding," Shep woofed, "we'll be here two more suns." He shuffled his paws closer to his chest and tried again to stand. This time, he managed to rise to his paws.

"See?" he yipped, wincing with every breath. "All better."

Callie watched his trembling legs with wide eyes and pricked ears. "Your chest is leaking," she barked.

Shep looked between his legs. Red drops fell from his fur. "It'll stop," he woofed. He took a step forward; his legs gave out and he landed snout-first in the sand.

Boji licked one of the cuts and whimpered. "I don't think another sun or two is going to do it."

Pumpkin looked down the beach, then back at Shep, then at the beach, all the while trembling. "I don't mean to be the flea in every dog's coat," she moaned, "but the humans are going back to their dens. Every heartbeat we stay makes it less likely our families will be at the shelter when we arrive."

The pack began to whimper. Shep smelled their fear of losing their families forever, but also their anxiety at the thought of having to leave him. He had to make the decision for them.

"You go on," he barked. "I'll follow your scent in a few suns."

Oscar strutted to the center of the pack. "No way," he barked. "We wait until you're better." He gave Pumpkin a cool stare, complete with a one-eyed squint. "He's our alpha — our champion. We don't leave without him."

"Fuzz stay," the cat meowed.

"We all stay," barked Daisy, stepping up to stand beside Oscar. "We're a pack." She looked down at him like a proud dam. Oscar smiled up at her, tail happily whipping in circles.

The other dogs waved their tails in agreement.

"Of course we stay," woofed Callie, smiling.

Pumpkin looked at the long stretch of beach and whimpered, then threw herself onto her belly.

Zeus hobbled down from the nearest pile of wreckage.

"He can use the wagon," the boxer barked. He limped across the sand, holding his injured paw against his chest. In his jaws he held what looked like an orange balloon.

Shep immediately scented for what treachery Zeus was plotting. He smelled nothing. The other dogs seemed just as wary. All except the pup.

"How will you walk?" yipped Oscar, padding toward Zeus.

Zeus spat the balloon on the sand. It was a strange balloon — it wasn't round, but rather tube shaped and about the length of a snout. Zeus gritted his teeth and jammed his hurt paw into its center.

"See," he grumbled. "Better than a wagon." He took a step forward and the bright orange tube held his weight.

Oscar's tail began to wag ecstatically. "You wanted to help Shep. That's why you were away all night!" he yipped. "I knew you were a good dog!" The pup leapt at Zeus's nose, licking the air.

Zeus grimaced and ducked away from the bouncing brown snout. "I didn't want to ride in the wagon anymore," he grunted. "It's rubbing the fur from my skin. I was going to leave it here no matter what."

Callie raised an eyebrow and gave Zeus a once-over sniff, complete with snaggletoothed smirk. "If you aren't going to use it," she woofed finally, "then I see no reason not to load Shep into it."

Daisy strutted over to the wagon and snuffled along its every surface. "It doesn't — *snort* — smell like he did anything to it," she barked. She kicked one of the fat wheels and the wagon rumbled down the sand toward the bubbling surf.

"What would I have done and why would I have done it?" Zeus snapped. "I just woofed that I was leaving it here with the rest of the trash. If Shep can't walk, he might as well use it."

Shep wanted to run over to Zeus and roll him in the sand. There *was* some of the old Zeus left in him! But one look at the scowl on Fuzz's muzzle kept Shep where he lay — that, and the fact that he couldn't stand.

Pumpkin burst up from her sand nest, spraying white grit everywhere. "We're going home!" she howled.

We're going home, Shep thought.

CHAPTER 14
HOME SWEET...
PILE OF RUBBLE

The destroyed buildings along the beach were hard to tell apart — one pile of cracked stone and broken glass looked just like the next. But not even the world-crushing wave could wipe the scent of Pumpkin's home completely from the earth. She paused in the sand and took a long, deep sniff.

"Home," she snuffled. Then she dove headlong into the nearest space in the slabs of stone.

Shep barked for the group to stop. He flicked his tail for Fuzz to follow her. The cat bounded over the rubble and off the beach.

Boji spat the wagon's rope from her slobbery jowls and flopped, panting, in the sand; she and Dover had been taking turns pulling Shep down the beach onto the wagon. Though Shep hated being so useless, he had little choice in the matter. His sides still ached with every breath.

The others sat on the sand, ears pricked and noses open. After several heartbeats, Fuzz appeared on top of a cracked wall, nodded his head, and disappeared again.

"We're here," Shep woofed.

The dogs wound their way through the wreckage. It was as if what sand had been taken from the beach now coated the streets: Drifts formed against every wall and tree. Dead palm fronds and leaves covered the sand, along with the usual trash and den debris.

The terrain was bumpy as a water lizard's hide, which made moving the wagon even more difficult. Boji pulled from the front and Dover pushed with his head from behind. The others nosed aside what obstacles they could to give Boji and Dover a clear path.

Zeus hobbled past them, a smirk on his jowls. "Now you smell why I ditched the thing," he growled, wincing as he stepped on his balloon-paw.

Boji glanced at the boxer and raised her hackles, but kept her growl to herself. "It's almost like he wants us to hate him," she snuffled.

Shep tried to shift his weight in the wagon. "Maybe if I helped you to push with my hind legs?" he woofed.

Dover rested a paw on Shep's flank. "It's time to let this pack carry you, the way you've carried us all these suns."

Once they were away from the beach, the sand-and-trash dunes, broken stone, and glass thinned out. Pumpkin stood on an empty square of pavement in front of one of the piles that used to be a building, her snout on her chest.

"This was my den," she woofed. "I can take us to the shelter from here." She lifted her small rump and turned away from her old home.

"We don't have to go," Shep yipped, "if you want to take a few more heartbeats."

Pumpkin looked at the wreckage, then turned away again. "For what? Everything I loved is no longer here." She loped down the street, hopping over the larger bits of glass that littered the stone.

The little show dog led them down block after ruined block. Some buildings were washed away entirely; others looked almost untouched except for the odd broken window or shard of wood sticking out of a wall; however, everything smelled of the wave. A salty rot wafted from every door and window.

They crossed over a wide expanse of water on a narrow bridge of roadway. Chunks of the road were missing, and they had to bump and hop over the parts that remained. At one place, the road had completely collapsed onto the spit of land beneath it. The pavement ended and there was nothing but a drop of several stretches to the dirt below. What remained of the section of street led like a ramp up from the dirt to the rest of the bridge.

Fuzz was the first to reach the broken edge of the street. "Watch step," he hiss-barked, then dropped off the cliff.

"Fuzz!" Shep yelped. Boji dragged him to the edge.

Fuzz landed on his paws, some seven stretches below. He looked back up at Shep's stricken muzzle. "What problem?" he meowed, licking a paw and running it over his ear.

Rufus trotted to the wagon's side. "Don't even *think* that I'm jumping this," he grumbled, then glared meaningfully at Callie.

Callie peered over the edge of the road. "No," she woofed. "The cat was lucky. I don't think even Shep at his best could make this jump." She glanced around, then at each of the dogs. "Okay, we swim."

"Swim?" Daisy snorted. Her short fur trembled on her back.

"Yes," Callie barked. "Like we did across the canal."

"When we lost Cheese?" Boji whimpered.

Callie stood tall, ears up and tail stiff. "We are nearly home," she barked. "I know this bridge. And we don't have to swim far." She trotted back a few stretches along the roadway. "We jump off here into the water, and then just swim onto the land and walk up that slab of roadway."

"Jump here?" cried Pumpkin. "That's almost — my fur, it's a million stretches from the roadway to the water!" She shivered so hard her fur vibrated into a cloud of white.

"Oh, Great Wolf," Callie sighed. She hopped onto the edge of the roadway and plummeted off the bridge.

"Callie!" Shep howled. Boji wheeled him closer to the side of the road. Callie dropped, legs stretched in front of her, and then burst into the water with a huge splash. *Please be all right*, Shep mumbled to himself.

Callie's small head sputtered to the surface. "See?" she grunted between pants. "Piece of jerky." She began paddling for the island under the bridge.

Shep licked his jowls, trying to take on a more alpha-like look before barking to the others. Callie's fearlessness shocked him still — he wouldn't have jumped off that bridge for an entire bag of treats.

He turned to his pack, whose muzzles betrayed their fears. Only Zeus wore a different look — his constant grimace of disdain.

Shep pushed himself up off his chest.

Boji put her paws on the wagon to hold it steady. "Are you sure you want to do this?" she woofed.

Gingerly placing his paws on the pavement, Shep snorted to clear his snout. "We either jump off this bridge or head back to the beach. I promised to get you all to the shelter, and that's where I'm going."

The dogs licked their jowls and sniffed the edge of the roadway. Only Zeus moved. As he passed, he cocked an eyebrow at Shep, then he dove off the bridge and splashed into the water below.

"Ha-roo!" Oscar cried, running for the edge. "I'm coming, Zeus!"

"Oscar, wait!" Shep barked. The pup couldn't swim!

Oscar plummeted off the precipice. Shep limped to try to catch his scruff but was too slow. When he got to the edge, however, he saw something amazing. Zeus paddled right under Oscar and caught the pup in his jaws like a tossed Frisbee.

What do you know? Shep thought, smiling.

The other dogs watched as Zeus swam with Oscar

between his jowls, then placed the pup gently on the shore.

Zeus dragged his own body out of the water. "Don't try that again," he snapped at Oscar.

The pup's tail wagged in huge circles and a smile broke out across his tiny snout. "I knew you were a good dog!" he barked. Oscar looked up at the pack with an I-woofed-you-so smirk on his muzzle.

"Maybe there's hope for the boxer yet," yipped Ginny, ears and tail raised in surprise.

Even Fuzz kept himself from spitting at Zeus when he passed on the way up the ramp.

Shep ordered Pumpkin to climb onto Dover's back, since she wouldn't jump on her own. Boji pushed the wagon off the edge of the street so it landed on the dirt below, and then every dog jumped. The water felt like a paw-thrust to the gut, but Shep survived the drop and swam, sputtering, to the spit of land. As the pack shook the water from their coats, Callie howled, "Let's get to that shelter!"

Once off the long bridge, Pumpkin turned down a side street, away from the cold winds. The buildings began to look eerily familiar.

"By Lassie's golden coat," cried Ginny, "we're home!" She bolted down an alley.

"We have to stay together!" Callie barked. But it was no use. Boji and Rufus raced after her.

"We'd better follow," Shep woofed.

Dover nodded his head and wheeled the wagon after the others.

It was only a few blocks to where the old building stood. It was still yellow and a few of the white, ornate balconies clung to its front, but for the most part, it was destroyed. Shep remembered the howling wind that broke Zeus's wall, the terrifying darkness when El Vator stopped so suddenly, when the roof was torn from the stairwell and Virgil pulled him back from oblivion.

Dover and Boji sat side by side, and the old timer licked Boji's golden head. Ginny howled miserably, leaving Rufus, of all dogs, to offer her a comforting woof. Daisy and Oscar considered the building, but not with sadness — Shep guessed maybe Daisy hadn't loved the place, and Oscar — well, he hadn't lived there long.

Zeus spat on the stone. "Good riddance," he snarled.

"That's my *home* you're spitting on," Ginny growled.

"I hate to woof you this," Zeus snapped, "but that pile of stones will never again be a home to any of us."

Ginny looked about ready to fight Zeus herself.

Shep shifted his chest, squeaking the wagon's wheels. "Pumpkin," he barked, "lead on."

The little fluff of white wagged her tail and trotted away down the street.

Something touched Shep's nose — out of all the scents of rot and salt and split wood and rusting metal, there came the unmistakable reek of wild dog. He looked at Zeus. *No, not him.* But Zeus had smelled it, too. His ears pricked forward and his head shot up for a better sniff of air.

Then Shep saw it — a shadow moving in the deeper shadows of the demolished building.

"We tracked your scent back here, Great Leader," the shadow snarled.

The pack did not run — Shep couldn't believe his nose, but not one of them smelled afraid.

"You get out of our home," growled Ginny — *Ginny!*

Rufus barked and bounced on his paws. "Get away, you brutes!"

The shadow stepped forward and not one but three wild dogs materialized in the light: two with brownish fur and one with a mottled whitish coat, the leader. Only the Great Wolf knew how many more skulked in the wreckage.

"You dogs best move on," growled Dover. He lowered his head and bared his teeth.

Callie planted her paws and snarled. Boji pounced on the dirt in front of her, barking sharply. Even Fuzz curled his spine and hissed and spat at the wild dogs. Shep was stunned to silence. What was this pack? Had he made fighters of them all?

The lead wild dog seemed as surprised as Shep at the ferocity coming from these pets. "We have no grudge with you, pets," the white barked. "We want the Great Leader. The rest can go."

"He's not your leader anymore," Oscar barked. "He's a part of our pack now."

The wild dogs panted. "He's no more a part of your pack than he was of ours," the white yipped. "More likely he's waiting for the first chance to kill you, the way he led us to the slaughter."

Zeus shifted slightly and the balloon on his paw popped.

"That's our problem now," yapped Daisy, kicking back with her hind claws. "You go, before we have to get feisty."

The lead dog snarled at Daisy and looked over the dogs, as if weighing the odds on fighting the whole pack of them.

Shep dragged his front paws out of the wagon and padded himself forward. He raised his head and ears and ended the discussion. "You have five heartbeats to get your tails out of my sight before I rip every one of them from your rumps."

The wild dogs scented his rage, the power burning inside him that even that sun's crushing pain and exhaustion couldn't put out. They stepped back.

"It's your hide that's going to be shredded," the white barked. The wild dogs slunk into the rubble. In heartbeats, the scent of them was gone from the street.

Zeus trembled slightly. "Why did you do that?" he grunted. "You could have been killed."

"You'd rather we left you to be torn apart by wild dogs?" snapped Callie.

"Zeus-dog killer, but no dog deserve that death," Fuzz meowed.

Boji strode forward. "And you're not all bad," she woofed. "We saw you rescue Oscar."

"Fuzz think Zeus-dog all bad," the cat hissed.

Daisy echoed Fuzz's disgust. "Let's not get fur-brained," she snorted. "He's a monster, but he's a part of this pack until we reach the shelter, and I defend my packmates."

Oscar leapt at the others' jowls. "I knew you could forgive us!" he yipped.

Boji licked his small snout. "If we don't forgive, how can we hope to move on?" She stood and waved her tail.

Zeus scowled and looked away from the pack. "You should have let them kill me," he snuffled.

"I could never have forgiven myself for that," Boji woofed. "You want to die so badly, do it yourself." She loped down the street. "You all coming, or am I the only one ready to see my family?"

CHAPTER 15
OUTSIDE THE OPEN DOOR

They walked, silent save for the squeak of the wagon's wheels. What could they woof? Their adventure was over. They were almost home. To bark that they were excited to see their families would have been to ignore how hard it was to think that they would never again be together as a pack. To yip that they would miss each other was too hard. So they remained silent. At least, that was how Shep explained his own inability to bark a woof.

Every few heartbeats, he glanced at Callie, and the sight of her stopped the beating of his heart. It had been nearly impossible to leave her behind at the boat, and he knew then that he would find her and see his friend again. But now who knew when, if ever, they would see each other's muzzles? Would their families try to rebuild in this drowned city, and if they did, would they live near enough to each other to even go to the same Park? How could he keep moving forward, knowing that every step took him closer to losing Callie and all his packmates forever?

"That's it," woofed Pumpkin. "That's the shelter." She waved her snout at a solid brick building.

They stopped as one dog, as if tugged by the same leash.

Shep raised his head and coughed. "It's been a good adventure," he woofed, then his bark cracked and he shut his snout.

Callie slumped beside him and leaned her head against the wagon. "It has," she snuffled.

"I won't miss the food," yipped Rufus.

"Oh, hush, you old hairball," woofed Ginny. She leapt onto Rufus's back and whimpered. "You loved every mouthful of squirrel you got your teeth on."

The two began licking each other's snouts and whimpering. Then every dog was in on it. Daisy snorted and howled about how much she loved every one of their ugly muzzles. Dover and Boji snuggled close, then pounced on Shep and his wagon. They dragged the small dogs close to them in a big pile of dog love. Oscar leapt into the mix and wriggled like a rat in the kibble pile. Fuzz strutted around the outside of the snuggle, rubbing against whatever fur was exposed and purring loudly.

Pumpkin sat down next to Zeus. "I feel like I missed out on something," she yipped.

"We did," Zeus snuffled.

The dog pile was too much for the wagon. Its wheels gave one final squeal, then collapsed. The pack stopped rolling and tumbling around one another. Slowly, they untangled. They separated into individual dogs. Shep lugged his body out of the ruined plastic. It was time to go home.

An old, bent, and broken fence separated the road from the shelter. It was a tall brick building with many parts and levels, though the section in front of the dogs seemed like a single huge den with a thin line of windows near its ceiling. Shep didn't smell or see any green men — maybe so long after the storm, they didn't care who or what came into the shelter.

The dogs squeezed one at a time through a large hole in the fence, then stood as a pack on the stretch of pavement that led to the shelter. A metal door was propped open, and the dogs smelled the warm, human scents wafting out of it.

"Thank you!" Pumpkin yipped. "Oh, thankyouthank-youthankyou!" she cried, leaping at Shep's jowls. "I never thought I'd make it back to my mistress, but you got me here." She turned to the rest of the pack. "And thank you all! I'll never forget our journey!" Then she bounded toward the shelter, barking for her mistress the whole way.

Ginny flounced over to Shep, planted her paws against his chest, and licked his nose. "I never believed that a dog could really be as wonderful as Lassie," she woofed. "But you, Shep, are that dog." She waved her tail to him and flopped onto the pavement.

"Good-bye, packmates," she woofed. "I never thought we'd make it, but just look at us! We survived! Huzzah!" She wagged her tail, then nodded her snout and trotted for the door.

Rufus snorted and raised his square snout. "It wasn't all great," he barked. "But it also wasn't all terrible." He sniffed his nose at Shep. "You were a good alpha."

Shep nodded his snout at Rufus. "And you weren't always a complete pain in the tail."

Rufus smiled for a heartbeat and wagged his stumpy tail. "Yes, well, neither were you," he woofed, then loped toward the door.

Dover turned to Shep. His eyes were deep and shining, and a smile played on his jowls. "You made this happen, pup," he woofed. He padded closer to Shep and waved his tail. "I know you didn't like those stories Oscar told, but you really were our champion. You saved the lives of a lot of pets, and you brought me out of a city-killing storm and back to my family." He licked Shep's snout. "Thank you, Shep."

"You're welcome," Shep yipped. He felt like if he woofed anything more, he might start howling and never stop.

Dover nodded his snout, turned, and trotted toward the door.

Happy shouts of humans and dogs echoed out of the shelter.

Boji's ears and tail lifted at the sound. She looked back at Shep. "What Dover said," she woofed. "And so much more, my friend. I'll never forget you."

Shep licked her snout. "You saved my life," he barked. "I owe you one."

"What does it matter anymore, who saved whom?" Boji smiled.

"How about you be my hero?" Shep yipped.

"Well, that works," she woofed. "Because you're mine."

With a final nuzzle of the snout, Boji loped toward the shelter door.

A young woman with limp black hair stepped out of the door and glanced around the pavement. Her eyes stopped at Daisy and she smiled.

Daisy nipped Oscar's hide; both of their tails were wagging.

"I guess we'd better head home," Daisy snuffled. She nodded her head at Shep and gave a flick of her knot-tail. "Alpha," she woofed, "I was always — *snort* — proud to serve you."

Shep nodded his snout to her. "You helped defend our pack," he said, tail waving. "I feel lucky to have had you as a packmate."

She trembled slightly, eyes wide, then snorted and kicked her back leg. "Let's go, pup!" she yipped and raced for the woman. Tears streamed down the human's cheeks as she flung her arms around Daisy's fat chest.

Oscar stayed frozen in his sit, staring up at Shep's muzzle. "What am I going to do without you?" he whimpered.

Shep limped next to him and licked his head. "You'll grow into a big dog," he woofed. "And become some other pup's hero, and he'll make up crazy stories about you because he loves you, and you'll love him back, no matter what fur-brained nonsense comes out of his snout."

"What if I never see you again?" Oscar woofed, his bark trembling.

"You'll always have the Storm Shaker," Shep yipped. "And the Great Wolf will watch over you."

Oscar flung himself against Shep's chest. "You'll always be my hero," he woofed.

Shep snuggled the pup's head with his muzzle. "You're a good dog, Oscar," he snuffled. "You'll always be in my heart."

The pup dropped to his paws and went over to Zeus. "Be the dog I see in you," he woofed.

Oscar then nuzzled against Callie, and she licked his head. Finally, he raced across the pavement, barking for his mistress to pet him, too.

Zeus watched the pup bound across the stone. "What did Oscar see?" he snuffled.

"He sees what I see," Shep woofed. "My old friend."

"I killed that Zeus," the boxer grunted. "What am I bringing back to my master?"

"You're bringing him his dog," Callie barked. "After all your master's been through, he deserves his dog back."

Zeus looked at them both and licked his jowls. "I guess he does." He turned to Shep. His eyes were huge, sad. "I'm sorry," he snuffled, "about everything."

"Me, too," Shep answered. "Maybe I'll see my old friend in the Park?"

Zeus winced a smile. "If I can ever find him again," he woofed. His stump tail waved.

"I'll be waiting."

Zeus tightened his jowls, then hobbled on his hurt paw across the pavement.

Shep, Callie, and Fuzz sat together, staring at the door.

"We made it home," Callie woofed.

"Yes," Shep yipped.

Callie stood. "I can't say good-bye to you." She licked her jowls. "So I'm not. We're walking in there together and demanding that our families stay in neighboring dens."

Shep smiled. "When did you learn to speak human?"

"I figure they'll just look at our determined muzzles and know," she yipped.

Shep licked Callie's head, snuggling her as best he could. "Meeting you was the best thing that ever happened to me," he woofed.

"All I did was get you into trouble," she snuffled.

"You saved my life," he barked, "in every way, every heartbeat of every sun, and every sun hereafter."

"You've been my life for so long," Callie whimpered. "What will I do without you?"

"Every night, when you look up at Frizzle next to the Great Wolf, know that I'm looking up there, too," Shep woofed. "That way, we can be together every night."

"Promise?"

Shep looked at Fuzz, then licked Callie's nose. "You're my best friend," he snuffled. "You're my home. We will always be together."

Callie smiled. "You're right," she yipped. She untangled herself from Shep's snuggle. "Are you ready to go to your human home?"

Shep licked his jowls. "Yes," he woofed, "I am."

CHAPTER 16
HOME

They walked through the door together, from the bright light of the sun to the stale air and darkness of the shelter. Humans sat hunched on low beds lined up, row upon row, throughout the huge space. Along the walls were bright stripes of color, and hoops drooping netting like the ones Shep's boy used to play under. Dim lights fizzed on the ceiling and the whole place reeked of socks.

Shep heard the happy yips and barks of his former packmates echoing throughout the space. *They found their families*, he thought happily. Some humans pushed past Shep to the door with smiles on their faces, only to turn back into the shelter, mouths slack and faces stricken. Shep wondered which of these was Higgins's master, or Virgil's, or Snoop's. He wanted to lick their hands and explain what happened, but he had to leave the granting of such comfort in the paws of the Great Wolf.

Callie's nose hit the ground. Shep followed her curly tail as she snuffled between the rows of beds. He needed to make sure she was safe before he went his own way. Fuzz followed close on his tail.

The room hummed with life. Shep saw how the humans had tried to make dens out of these flat, narrow cots the way his pack had scratched the pillows together in the boat. Blankets were tented over poles to create walls and beds were pushed together to mark where a family nested. As Shep passed, the people looked at him not with fear — he smelled no anxiety from them — but with wonder, like he was the Great Wolf himself visiting from the sky. A few reached out tentative fingers, desperate for the feel of fur. Shep wondered how many of them had left dogs behind and how many would return home to find they'd lost their homes and their pets with them.

"Callie!"

A little girl sprang over a bed, wild hair whipping behind her.

"My girl!" yipped Callie, tail waving.

The girl wrapped her thin arms around Callie. Callie leapt at her face, licking her over and over. The girl mumbled things in a soft, sweet voice as she stroked Callie's fur. Shep saw tears running down her face.

After a few heartbeats, the girl noticed Shep. She smiled·and said something. She stretched out a hand. Not wanting to scare the girl, Shep waved his tail and lowered his head. The girl wiggled her fingers, and he chanced a quick lick of her fingertips. The girl smiled.

Callie was panting and wagging her tail so hard her rump waved with it. The girl hoisted Callie up into her arms and walked down a row of beds. Shep followed, not ready to let Callie out of his sight.

The girl stopped at a sagging bed piled with bags. On it sat a tired, sad-looking woman. When she saw Callie, she burst into tears. Shep wondered if she was sad to see Callie, but then the woman stretched her arms out, took Callie from the girl, and hugged Callie to her chest. The girl wrapped her arms around the two of them and Shep saw that a family had just been made whole.

The three untangled themselves. Callie sat on her girl's lap as the mother examined Callie's paws and face. Fat tears rolled down her cheeks and she kept mumbling the same sounds with a trembling smile on her lips.

Callie looked back at Shep, eyes warm and happy, a smile on her jowls.

"Go find your family," she yipped. "You brought me home, just like you promised."

"I'll see you tonight?" Shep woofed.

"Every night," she said.

Shep padded forward. The girl thought he was coming to woof with her, so she stroked his scruff and said something in a soft voice. Shep licked Callie's head, and she licked his nose. Then he turned and trotted away before he lost the strength to leave her. He heard Fuzz meow to her behind him, and Callie respond in cat-speak.

That crazy yapper, Shep thought to himself, smiling.

Shep scented the ground, as Callie had. For several rows, he smelled nothing, but then he caught a whiff of his boy. He followed the tiny trail of scent to a group of beds, but they were empty. No bags were piled alongside the cots; an empty plastic bottle jutted from under a corner of the bare mattress; one white sock with a hole near the toe was caught under the bed's metal leg — it was the only remnant left of his boy.

Fuzz hopped onto the bed, his tiny nose twitching. "Smell strong," he hissed. "Boy here not long ago."

"Why would he leave?" Shep yipped.

"Maybe go home?" Fuzz meowed.

Home, Shep thought, a warm feeling rippling through his body.

"Let's go find him," Shep woofed.

They returned through the door, Shep shuffling along as fast as his broken body would let him. Once on the street, Shep tried to recall the path of wandering he and Callie had taken that sun — so long ago, cycles ago, in a different city entirely, it seemed. He knew they had turned away from the cold winds, and so he lumbered toward them, turning when necessary ever toward sunrise. He knew that much: that he lived toward the cold winds, toward sunrise.

This part of the city was still in the ruined state the storm had left it in. Hunks of trash remained strewn across the streets, wilted now after so many suns. Dead leaves and branches coated the sand piles so that they looked like huge, alien creatures snoozing in the sun. Buildings creaked and groaned as if impatient to tumble into the piles of broken stone they were destined to become.

Shep despaired of ever being able to find his home amidst all this destruction. But then he found a familiar-smelling building. Then another. Even the devastation of the wave could not raze every landmark. He turned one corner and recognized a building down the street. Fuzz loped in front of him, nosing the pointiest bits of rubble and sharpest scraps of metal from Shep's shambling path.

Shep's heart raced in his chest. He thought of what he would do once he got to his building. He would run up the stairs to his den and his family would be waiting inside. The woman would be holding a huge bowl of kibble laced with gravy and bits of meat. The man would have his hands on the boy's shoulders. The wave would certainly have washed away the mess Shep had made in the kitchen, so there would be no reason for any of them to be angry. His boy would run to him — of course he would — but Shep would not forget to say hello to the man and the woman. He would nose Fuzz in front of them and hopefully they would understand that Fuzz was a part of their family now.

Shep saw his street — one more block and he would be before his building. His paws burned against the stone and his breath came in ragged, painful pants, but he had to keep going. He was almost home. *I'm here, Boy!*

And then Shep saw that something was terribly wrong.

His den building, the one that smelled of all the humans who had lived there over the cycles, stood before him, but half of it was a crumbled pile of stones. The front wall ended a few stretches above Shep's head and the side wall, which had led to the alley, was completely missing. The stairwell rose like a curling stone and metal plant into the sky. Shep pawed at the door and it opened with a whine.

"Should Fuzz go in?" the cat mewed.

"No," Shep grunted. "There's nothing here for me now."

What fur-brained fantasy did he succumb to, thinking that his home would have been spared when every other building in this drowned city had been destroyed? Of course his home was gone. Of course his family left the shelter. Of course he'd been abandoned again.

The cat looked at Shep with his intense cat-eyes. He purred and nuzzled his head against Shep's leg. "Shep-dog not fuzz head to hope home survive," he meowed.

Shep wagged his tail. "This pile of stones isn't my home," he woofed.

The cat glanced up at him and purred louder.

Shep allowed his legs to rest, slumping into a sit against the door frame. "I guess we're forming that pack after all," Shep grunted. "Though we'd better wait until I can stand for more than a heartbeat before beginning recruitment."

Fuzz sat and wrapped his tail around his paws. "Shepdog give up so easy?" he meowed.

Shep sighed. Was it really giving up to admit that the storm had beaten him? Wasn't there some point at which struggling on was just completely fur-brained? How would he find his family now? They weren't at the shelter; their den had been washed away.

"I guess we could go to the dog catchers back at the big kennel," Shep woofed. "Maybe my boy will come looking for me there?"

He glanced at Fuzz, and the cat nodded his head.

Shep sniffed the door frame, taking in that familiar scent one last time. "Good-bye," he snuffled.

The two friends padded slowly down the ruined street.

The sun was falling in the sky. Shep was realistic about how far he could travel, given his crippled condition:

It would take them at least two suns to reach the kennel. They needed to find a safe place to rest for the night.

"Fuzz find den," the cat meowed.

"I know a place," Shep woofed. "I'd like to see the old run one last time."

The Park opened off the street like a refuge from the stone. Some of its trees had fallen, but many still waved their branches in the breeze. Junk littered the grass; paper and plastic bags tumbled across the empty space like leaves. But even ruined, in the golden light of late midsun, Shep·could feel the power that this place once held for him. This was where he first felt happiness.

"Come on," Shep woofed. "We can sleep in the dog run."

They loped into the Park and over to the posts that marked the boundary of the old dog run. The metal mesh of the fence's walls was bent or missing. Even in his broken condition, Shep was able to hop over the scrap that remained into the enclosure.

The storm had washed away most of the obstacles in the run, though a few poles still jutted from the dirt. There was the corner where the water hose used to create a muddy swimming hole. And over there, the pole with the trash that always smelled of scat. Beside a bent stretch of fence was the palm tree Frizzle had tried to claim — toppled now —

"Fuzz see human on tree," the cat meowed.

Shep couldn't believe his nose, wouldn't believe it. He sniffed again, then hobbled and limped to the palm.

Shep stopped in front of the person — his boy. His boy sat on the broken trunk, his knees pulled up to his chest and arms around his legs. His head rested on his knees.

"Boy?" Shep woofed. His bark was tremulous and his tail waved.

The boy looked up. His face was dirty and sad. He looked older, like the two moons that had passed were more like cycles. And then a smile cracked across his lips and his eyes opened wide.

"Shep!" he cried, falling forward off the tree and tackling Shep. "Oh, Shep!" he said, hugging Shep's neck like he would never let him go.

"Boy!" Shep woofed. "I can't believe I found you!" He licked the boy's face, wanting to clean it of all its dirt, of all the pain he saw written across the boy's skin.

The boy sobbed, soaking Shep's fur with his tears. His fingers clenched Shep's scruff and he muttered into Shep's fur. Shep could tell the boy was unloading to him all that he'd been through over the last moon-cycles. And Shep knew now that he could handle anything the boy needed him to hold.

"I'm here now, Boy," Shep snuffled. "I will protect you."

It's what an alpha does.

EPILOGUE

The dogs were on her the heartbeat Pumpkin set paw in the Park.

"You have to bark what happened next!" one particularly boisterous Boston terrier puppy yipped.

"Great Wolf!" Pumpkin barked. "Give me a chance to take off my leash, DeeDee!"

The terrier hopped back, bouncing with excitement. "New story!" she cried. "New story!"

The small dogs, and even some of the big ones from the other side of the fence, collected in the shade of the giant banyan tree. They sat or lay down in the grass, licking their chops and watching Pumpkin as she settled herself near the base of the trunk.

Pumpkin liked to howl her tales under the spreading

branches of the old banyan. It had somehow survived the storm, as had Pumpkin and her stories. Though so much had been destroyed and then torn apart and dragged away and built over and remade, this tree stood as a reminder of the drowned city that was.

"Now," Pumpkin woofed, "where did we leave off?"

She had barked the tales so many times by this age, she often forgot her place in any given woofing. But she was an old timer now and such things were becoming more common. A chew toy she swore she buried under the pink throw pillow would vanish from existence; she forgot to eat her kibble all morning and would find herself suddenly starving in the early afternoon. *It's such a bother, growing old.*

"Shep and the dog pack had just crossed the canal and fought off the giant lizards!" barked a bright-eyed pup — a mix of breeds that had mushed into something uniquely adorable.

"Oh, yes," Pumpkin yipped. "So, are you all ready to hear about what happened when they met Blaze?" She smiled at the group of snouts surrounding her, all eyes glued to her muzzle.

Pumpkin had started woofing the stories as a way to connect with the other dogs on the show circuit. Over the cycles, her tales became more famous than her flowing tail! Dogs would howl from across the grooming area for her to bark the legend of the Great Wolf or some other story. But she had long since retired from the show circuit, having won enough trophies to fill a whole wall in her mistress's den. Now, she had to admit, she barked the tales in the Park to recapture a little of that attention. It was always nice to get back in the spotlight.

"Please!" DeeDee whined. All the others echoed her excitement with howls and wagging tails.

"Well, huddle closer, dear packmates," Pumpkin barked, clearing her snout, "and I'll tell you the tale of Shep and Callie and all the other fearless Dogs of the Drowned City. . . ."

YOU NEVER KNOW WHAT WILL HAPPEN TOMORROW

Tomorrow is a whole new day . . .
Read on for a preview of
Tomorrow Girls #1: Behind the Gates.

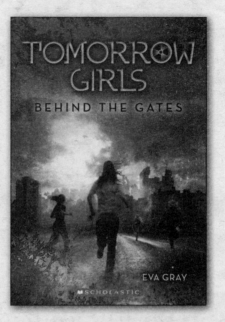

On the first day of school we scramble to find the classes on the schedules we've been given. My first class is English. The teacher, Sasha, doesn't even greet us. "Copy this into your notebooks, ladies" is all she says. Then she turns to the old-style blackboard and picks up a white stick of something I don't recognize. With rapid movements she covers the blackboard in notes, all written in an artful, curved script. My grandmother wrote like this, I recall. Otherwise almost everyone prints these days.

Glancing around the room, I notice that everyone is having a hard time taking notes without their laptops or notepads. I actually get hand cramps from writing with the pencil provided on my desk. And forget using an eraser! They don't even work!

My notebook winds up full of scratch-outs and scribbles. It's a complete mess and I hope no one will check it.

The rest of our morning is spent on other familiar subjects — social studies, algebra, and science.

"Don't you think it's weird that all the English and social studies books are from before 1980?" Evelyn points out as we walk to our next class.

"The school is old, and it's probably hard to get supplies," Maddie suggests. "You know how hard it is to get anything since the War started."

"She's right," I say. Mom and Dad told me that back in the day, there were huge stores that sold tons and tons of cheap stuff. Everything was affordable because it was all made in countries where people didn't have any rights and no one made enough money.

But honestly, I might not have even noticed the old textbooks if Evelyn hadn't pointed them out. I like my classes — a lot. The teachers seem pretty nice, so far. They're all young women with various accents and nationalities — except for Mrs. Brewster, who doesn't have any kind of accent and doesn't teach any courses. She's just in charge.

We're supposed to call all the teachers by their first names, like Devi and Emmanuelle and Sasha. It's hard to get used to, especially since things are pretty formal here otherwise. But the only last name we use is Mrs. Brewster's — and no one knows her first name. Evelyn calls her "Bunny" as a joke sometimes.

In the afternoon we have speech and debate. After that we have Emmanuelle for outdoor survival skills. I know afternoons will be my favorite. I'm not sure which of these two classes I love the most.

In every class we're told that we are part of the New Society. It doesn't take me long to figure out that in the New Society we will be the privileged elite who will be expected to lead the masses when the War is over. Our teachers keep referring to us as the *future of the country.*

"That's kind of obnoxious, don't you think?" Maddie says to me at dinner. "Why should we be the future of the country just because we can afford to go to this school? If you think about it, it's offensive."

I shrug — I kind of like the idea. It gives me a feeling of having a serious purpose. I'd never felt like that in school before. Mostly all of it had seemed unimportant. All I could think was, *Why do we even have to know this stuff?* At CMS, I don't feel that way.

"Of course it's offensive," Maddie insists, replying to my shrug. "If your parents hadn't paid for me to be here, my parents couldn't have afforded it."

My eyes dart around quickly, making sure no one is listening. "Shh," I warn.

Maddie lowers her voice. "Now I'm a 'future leader' because I'm here. If I couldn't afford to be here, who would I be? A big nobody?"

"But you *are* here," I remind her.

"That's not the point."

I know it's not the point, but this is a touchy subject and I want to get off it. "Well, I'm just happy we're here," I say. "And you should be, too."

Evelyn sits down at our table. "I have to ask you guys something about science," she says. "Don't you think it's odd that we'll be learning an awful lot about starting fires, building explosives, and making poisonous gases?"

"I had fun building that fire today," I say.

"Sure, it was fun," Evelyn admits, "but don't you

think it's a little weird that tomorrow we're going to learn how to blow stuff up?"

I only shrug, again, because I think that's going to be really interesting, too. For the first time in my life I enjoy science class. Maybe it is a little strange, but then, what's normal anymore?